Pra [barcode: D0776123] iams

DIANE WILLIAMS

excitability

SELECTED STORIES  1986-1996

DALKEY ARCHIVE PRESS

The selected stories in this collection were published separately in three
volumes under the titles:

This Is About the Body, the Mind, the Soul, the World, Time, and Fate by
Grove Weidenfeld, 1990; *Some Sexual Success Stories Plus Other Stories
in Which God Might Choose to Appear* by Grove Weidenfeld, 1992; *The
Stupefaction* by Alfred A. Knopf, Inc., 1996.

Library of Congress Cataloging-in-Publication Data:

Williams, Diane
Excitability : selected stories / by Diane Williams. — 1st ed.
p.   cm.
ISBN 1-56478-197-6 (pb : alk. paper)
I. Title.
PS3573.I44846E93   1998
813'.54—dc21   98-22015
CIP

This publication is partially supported by a grant from the
Illinois Arts Council, a state agency.

Dalkey Archive Press
Illinois State University
Campus Box 4241
Normal, IL 61790-4241

Printed on permanent/durable acid-free paper and
bound in the United States of America.

Note on cover art: John Graham, American, 1881-1961, Untitled (study for La
Donna Ferita), crayon and pencil on yellowed tracing paper, 1945, 39.7 x 26.4 cm,
The Lindy and Edwin Bergman Colleciton, 135.1991
photograph © 1998, The Art Institute of Chicago, All Rights Reserved.

Contents

From *Some Sexual Success Stories Plus Other Stories in Which God Might Choose to Appear*

From *The Stupefaction*

This Is About the Body, the Mind, the Soul, the World, Time, and Fate

Lady

She said *please*. Her face looked something more than bitter, with hair which it turned out was a hat, which came down over her ears, which was made of fake fur, which she never removed from her head. She had glasses on. Everything she wore helped me decide to let her in.

She wore flat black patent-leather shoes with pointed toes, with black stockings, wrinkled at the ankles, with silver triangles set in on top of the toes of the shoes to decorate them, and she had on a long black coat, and she was shorter than I am.

Her skin was a bleak sort of skin, and there was no

beauty left in her—maybe in her body.

I felt that this lady is fast, because she was at the place where I keep my red rotary-dial phone before I was, after I said, "The phone is in here."

She said, "I know the number."

Sitting on the arm of my sofa, she dialed while her knees were knocking into and tipping back onto two legs my too-small table, which my phone sits on, and my oversized brass lamp, which sits on the table too, with the huge shade, might have crashed. The lamp was clanging, ready to go. She got it back.

She said, *"Merla!"* into the phone receiver.

I knew it—she must have known it—Merla knew it too, that Merla was only a matter of one hundred to two hundred yards from my house, because this woman I had let in, she had told me right off the house number she was looking for. She was telling Merla that it was *impossible* to get to her, that there was no way on earth, that she had kept on running into this east-west street.

"A nice picture," she said to me.

She had gotten herself up. She was looking at all of those men dressed for one of the dark-age centuries, marching through foliage, trekking around a hunched-up woman at a well, with their weird insignias on their chests, that nobody I know can figure out, with their faces—version after version of the same face.

She said, "I have a"—something something—"reproduction—" I cannot remember the dates or the royal reign to which she referred, when she was toying with this miniature chair that I have, grabbing it by its arm, and swiveling it on the clubbed foot of one leg, as she was leaving, after everything had been agreed upon with Merla. She would not be getting out of her car for Merla. Merla would meet her at the corner. Merla would.

She, the lady, must have been curious or put off by the jumble of dirty things at my front door that I suppose she first noticed when she was leaving, or by the splendor of my living room just off from the jumble. She missed going inside of it to see what was going on in each of the pictures in there.

What this woman had done to me was incalculable, and she had done it all in a period of time which had lasted no more than five minutes, which so many others have done, coming in here only for the telephone, because I had waved at her while she was shouting at Merla, I had said, "Would it help you to know the number of *this* house?"

Then I had told this little person my wrong address, not because I wanted to, nor because of any need on my part to make up a lie.

I said 2-7-0 which is way off the track, except for two digits, but I had rearranged them, the 7 and the 0, but I did not know I had done that. All that I knew was that I had done something unforgivably uncivil.

It was a lapse to reckon with. I took her into my arms, so that she could never leave me, and then jammed her up into the corner with the jumble by the front door and held her in there, exhausting myself to keep her in there. I didn't care. It hurt her more than it hurt me, to be a lady.

Violence is never the problem. Love at first sight is.

The Nature of the Miracle

The green glass bottle rolled into, rolled out of my arms, out of my hands, and then exploded, just as it should, when it hits our bluestone floor, and spreads itself, and sparkling water, on the territory it was able to cover from our refrigerator to the back door.

The bottle used to fit tightly in my hand, easily, by the neck, and the way one thing leads to another in my mind, this means I should run away from my marriage.

I should run to the man who has told me he does not want me. He does not even like me. Except for once he took me, and my head was up almost under his arm, my neck was,

and my hand went up his back and down his back, and he cop-
ied what I did to him on my back with his hand, so that I
would know what it would be like, I would have an idea, and
then I could run home to my marriage afterward, which is
what I did before, after we were done with each other; and
the way one thing leads to another in my mind, this means I
should run to the man for more of it, but the way one thing
leads to another, first I will tell my husband, "I would not
choose you for a friend," then I will run to the other man, so
that I can hear him say the same thing to me.

This is unrequited love, which is always going around so
you can catch it, and get sick with it, and stay home with it, or
go out and go about your business getting anyone you have
anything to do with sick, even if all that person has done is
push the same shopping cart you pushed, so that she can go
home, too, and have an accident, such as leaning over to put
dishwasher powder into the dishwasher, so that she gets her
eye stabbed by the tip of the bread knife, which is drip-drying
in the dish rack. It is a tragedy to lose my eye, but this heroism
of mine lasted only a matter of moments.

Orgasms

I swear I did not have anything of hers except for my dark idea of her which I have been keeping to myself until now.

Even better than catching my own husband in the act with her, I opened my mouth, but I left her probably forever, before I made a statement.

She was presiding with her face flattened by some shadow. Her shoulders and her arms, and all across the front of her also were gray which was what made the idea of her dark.

I saw the top half of her blotted out—more than half of

what was behind her—nothing more, except some of her black hair curled away up into the—the way hair will, the way hers did. What of it?

If you care, it was like, like going by her like I was this big fish swallowing a big big fish whole, but because I am bigger, and what of it?

She kept on having orgasms with my husband.

The orgasms—where do they go?—crawling up into—as if they could have—up into—dying to get in, ribbed and rosy, I saw seashells were the color mouths should be, or the nipples of breasts, or the color for a seam up inside between legs, or, for I don't care where. Since they are pretty is why I collect them.

All American

The woman, who is me—why pretend otherwise?—wants to love a man she cannot have. She thinks that is what she should do. She should love a man like that. He is inappropriate for some reason. He is married.

When she thinks of the man, she thinks *force*, and then whoever has the man already is her enemy—which is the man's wife.

The woman makes sure the man falls in love with her. She has fatal charm. She can force herself to have it. Then she tells the man she cannot love him in return. She says, "You are in the camp with the enemy."

Of course, the woman knew the man was sleeping with the enemy before she ever tried to love him, and the word *enemy* gives joy—the same as I get when the wrong kind of person calls me *darling*, as when my brother says, "Okay," to me, "goodbye, darling," before he hangs up the phone, after we have just made some kind of pact, which is what we should do, because I have to force myself to love the ones I am supposed to love, and then I have to force myself on the ones I am not supposed to love.

I got my first real glimpse of this kind of thing when I was still a girl trying to force myself on my sister. I didn't know what I was doing until it was obvious. We were in the back seat of the family car. The car had just been pulled into the garage. The others got out, but we didn't. I thought I was not done with something. Something was not undone yet— something like that—and I was trying to kiss my sister, and I was trying to hug my sister, and she must have thought it was inappropriate, like what did I think I was a man and she was a woman?

I must have been getting rough, because she was getting hysterical. I remember I was surprised. I remember knowing then that I was applying force and was getting away with it.

The Uncanny

Her silver hair ornament was awfully big. I saw a great emerald-diamond ring. I saw the platter of steak tartare leave its position near me and then dive away into the party crowd on the back lawn. Then I saw my own husband having the meat on a Ritz cracker. I saw it in his hand next to his mouth. I drank my iced drink while it was changing color from a deep gold color that had satisfied me deeply to a gold color that certainly did not.

I asked Mrs. Gordon Archibald what she would have done with all of the people if it had rained. I gave her a suggestion for an answer she could give me which was an antisocial answer. She had a different antisocial answer for me of her own.

After this, my husband and I went off to a dinner club where there was dancing, where a woman touched my earring. She got it to move, saying, "These are buckets!"

My husband said to me while I was swooning in his arms, "Why are all the longest dances the draggiest?"

I took this to mean that he has not loved me for a very long time. Everything means something, or it does not. I have expressed an opinion. Every effect has a source that is not unfamiliar. It's all so evil.

The Kind You Know Forever

I had just met them—the brother and the sister who had fucked each other to see what it would be like. And then they said—either he said or she said—that it was like fucking a brother or a sister, so they never did it again.

That they had fucked each other was gossip intended to warn me away from the brother at the party where I watched the sister spread her legs carelessly, so that anyone—for instance, me—could look up her skirt to see darkness when she was sitting on the sofa.

Her husband was next to her—a thick man in a suit which was too small for him or was just under strain. The suit was ripped, I could see, under the arm at the seam. He had his arm up and around his wife, the sister who had fucked her brother.

I wondered if the husband knew, if he knew everything about her or not. I wondered as I watched her legs, her knees bump together, and then spread apart, and I kept my eye on him, while we were sitting around, but I forgot about the husband altogether while we ate. It was a fine meal we had.

And after that meal, the woman who had tried to warn me away from the brother took me aside. We went together from her kitchen to her bathroom. It was her party, and she led me there, and she closed the door. She said, "Look, you be careful." She said, "He's knocked up six girls."

And I said, "What does that mean?"

Then I saw how her long dark hair moved back and forth on either side of her head while she was moving her head, while her eyes were moving around, but not looking at me, while she was figuring me out. She said, "He got them all pregnant."

And I said, "And he didn't care what happened to them?"

"Yes. That's it," she said. "Now you be careful."

She must have known then her party was almost over, because there wasn't much time left after that. She handed out little wrapped gifts in such a hurry at the door, when we were all saying goodbye—it was such a hurry—I didn't get to see where she was getting all of her gifts from. All of a sudden there was just a gift in my hand, as I was going out the door. At the end of a party, I had never gotten a gift before, not since I was a girl, and then we thought we deserved those gifts. So now, something was turned around.

The gift she gave me was a cotton jewel pouch, in a bright shade of pink, made in India, which snapped shut.

I left the party with the sister-fucker. It was logical. We were near to the same age and we were both pretty for our kind, which must have mattered. Let me not forget to add that his sister was pretty, and that her husband was handsome, and that the woman who gave the party was pretty, and that her husband was handsome too.

The sister-fucker and I had both come to the party alone, and it was his idea that we should leave together. First we stopped at a bar, where we both had some drinks. I held onto a matchbook. I turned it by its four corners while he told me everything he was in the mood to tell me about his life, so that I felt I had known him forever.

Then I told him everything I was in the mood to tell him about my life—everything that mattered. I couldn't say now what that was. Then he said, "Write your phone number on the matchbook," which I did.

I asked him, "Should I write my name too?"

And he said, "No, not your name, just your number."

We were at the door in darkness ready to leave the bar

when I gave him the matchbook. He gave me a kiss. He pressed hard on my mouth for the kiss and then I was waiting to see what would happen next.

I still see him backing away covered in the shadows. Then he pushed his hands up into his hair. One of his hands was still holding the matchbook so that the whole matchbook went up into it too, sliding under. He was pushing so hard up into his hair with both hands on either side of his head, that he was pulling the skin of his face up and back. He was turning his eyes into slits. He was making his nose go flat. His mouth at the corners was going up.

I didn't know if he was playing around with me, if he was angry, or if he was trying to figure something out. I didn't ask, What does that mean? Now I think it meant he really cared, but it never made a difference. I have fucked him and fucked him and fucked him, and I have felt all that hair on his head in my hands plenty of times.

The Hero

My aunt was telling me about them coming to get them after I brought back the second helping of fish for me and the vegetables she asked for—the kind that have barely been cooked that look so festive, even with the film of dressing that dulls them down. I didn't want her to have to get up to get her own, not since she's been sick.

My aunt was saying, "They're going to get us. Hurry! Hurry! They're going to kill us!" after I put the vegetables down for her.

She said, "Your mother was a baby in my mother's arms." She said, "I get out of breath now when I eat. Jule says I'm not the same since I was sick. He says to me, You've changed."

"You haven't changed," I said.

She said, "They had the wagon loaded. They had the cow. You know they had to take the cow to give the children milk to drink. They were going to hide! To hide! To hide in the woods! And then Jule said, I've got to go!

"Everything was loaded. They said, Hurry! They're coming! They're going to kill us! But Jule said, I've got to go! So they said, Do it! Do it! Hurry! So then Jule said, But I need *the pot!*"

"He said that?" I said. "I never heard that story. Does my mother know that story?"

My aunt smiled, which I took then to be no. And my mother wasn't there, so I couldn't rush to her, I couldn't tell her, Do you know the story about your family? How you were going to be killed? How Uncle Jule stopped everything to go?

Uncle Jule appeared then. He was wearing a white golf hat.

My aunt said, "*You could put it in your hat.*" She said that to Jule. I don't remember why she said that—*You could put it in your hat.*

He must have said something first to her about her vegetables—could he take home what she wasn't going to eat? Maybe that was it.

Uncle Jule was blinking and smiling when she said, *You could put it in your hat.* He was blinking faster than anyone needs to blink.

Cauliflower was what my aunt left on her plate. It looked to me like some bleached-out tree.

Ten Feet from It

His body shifts and gets closer to me in a shady part of our house where hardly any natural light can get to, unless a bathroom door is open fully. At no time during this is he more than two or three feet away from me, and always he keeps turning to me so I can see how he is, not to prove anything to me. He is not the kind to do that. I am.

He is my son, one of them.

My other son broke down for me later in this day, my husband the same, a few days ago, my brother later in this day. My mother said to me, "I am not with it," just after we both witnessed my brother.

I can put the sight of any of them up in front of myself again anytime I want to: my son in grief because I would not believe that he really is; my other son the same; my husband, when he told me, "That broke the ice," after what I had said to him—whatever it was; my brother, as he was telling me his life is at stake.

My mother, her grief is the most overwhelming.

She was sitting with her Old Testament which has such tissue-thin pages and she was making the pages make a noise when I found her.

The biggest, broadest window of her house was in front of her, where she was sitting with the open book. I have the same dark red leather-bound version of the text.

I said to my mother, "Let me kiss you." I was up close to her, my hands on her forearms to get closer to her, but I did not get closer. For some reason she was standing at that time, perhaps to let me try, and then she was down, sitting at the desk which had been my desk when I was a girl.

She was looking at the shake-shingled roof, at the plum tree, at the trees all pushed together beyond it, at the violent plunging-down that our land takes below that window where one of my sons killed himself, because he was trying to keep my other sons from killing themselves, just about ten feet from the plum tree. He was shouting at those boys, or he was talking softly to those boys, who were talking softly to him, so all of them had to lean so far over to hear what they had to hear, so one of them could die.

It is just a sight with the body of my mother in front of it.

I can refer to the window glass. I can refer to the sky which might as well be the sea.

I go down the stairs of my mother's house, satisfied and slowly.

I cannot get a sight up in front of me now of little boys or of grown-ups together, so that I can hear what they are saying, so that I would want to repeat what it was they were saying, so that what they have said would change everything once and for all.

Dropping the Masters

There was a clatting sound, for all this kissing, for all this copulation. My boys could get those Masters of the Universe up and onto the dresser top in one swoop up—*a kiss to the bride! a kiss to the bride!*—it was the only way they got them married, the way my youngest boy had decided they should get them married. One swoop down and then they could rock a pair and make those Masters copulate just as long as they wanted them to. Until I let my boys see me so that I saw the faces of I'm hot and I'm caught, and I saw the faces of this has got to stop—that's the way I saw them when they were stopping, when a hand was up with a Master, when a boy the height of our dog begging was up on his knees like he was handing out a bone.

I was going nowhere after I stopped them, just down the hall toward the bathroom, just stuck almost at the end of the top of our house so that of course I didn't want to stay there where I had no business being or intention, where I felt stupid and strange almost in the bathroom. Now their door was shut so that I could hear the sound of them, but I could get no meaning. I could hear rough scrubbing and more clatting and not know anything about it at all. But I was back in front of the shut door of their room and there was nowhere else I wanted to be more than watching again or just to know what they knew—to know everything about what they knew and so that is where I stood.

So then I opened their door.

But this time the stopping was not like the stopping before, it was an altogether different kind of stopping. This was how dare you with the Masters being deeply ground down I thought maybe so they would break because these Masters break.

What I got to see then was the sluggishness of let's do another thing—the turning away and then the boys hopping the Masters and then dropping them.

These Masters weren't broken, they were only done— and my boys were walking out on me, finished.

Baby

Nobody was getting up close to me, whispering, "Do you get a lot of sex?" Nobody was making my mouth fall open by running his finger up and down my spine, or anything like that, or talking dirty about dirty pictures and did I have those or anything like those, so I could tell him what I keep—what I have been keeping for so long in my bureau drawer underneath my cable-knit pink crew—so I could tell him what I count on happening to me every time I take it out from under there. Because it was a baby party for one thing, so we had cone paper hats and blowers, so we had James Beard's mother's cake with turquoise icing, and it was all done up inside with scarlet and pea-green squiggles, and the baby got toys.

Nobody was saying, "Everybody has slept with my wife, because everybody has slept with everybody, so why don't we sleep together?" so I could say at last, "Yes, please. Thank you for thinking of me." I would be polite.

Just as it was nothing out of the ordinary when the five-year-old slugged the eleven-year-old on the back and they kept on playing, looking as if they could kill for a couple of seconds. We didn't know why. And then the baby cried in a bloodthirsty way.

My husband sat stony-faced throughout. I don't think he moved from his chair once. What the fuck was wrong with him? He left the party early, without me; he said to get a little—I don't know how he was spelling it—I'll spell it *peace*.

I spoke to a mustached man right after my husband left. He was the first man all night I had tried to speak to. I know he loves sports. I said to him, "I think sports are wonderful. There are triumphs. It is so exciting. But first, you have to know what is going on."

Then my boy was whining, "Mom, I want to go home." He was sounding unbearably tired.

The baby's aunt said she'd take us. She didn't mind. She had to back up her car on the icy drive. She said, "I don't know how we'll get out of here," when we got into the car. "The windows are all fogged up." She said, "I don't think I can do it." She opened the window and poked her head out. She said, "I don't think so."

When she closed the window, we went backward terrifically fast. I don't know how she knew when to spin us around into the street. It was like being in one of those movies I have seen the previews for. It was like watching one of those faces on those people who try to give you the willies. It was like that, watching her—while she tried to get us out.

Cloud

How it was in the aftermath of it, was that her body was in the world, not how it had ever been in the world before, in her little room or in *their* rooms—the people who owned the rooms—or at least were managing the rooms, their hallways, or the stairwell, which was not hers either, that she went through and through and through. A man laughed at her for what she had said, and then someone had brought her to this bed.

She looked at the bed stacked high with so many coats and she decided, It all stops here.

She was clearing up to be helpful before she left, steering

herself, when she saw her purse go flying and then it fell down into a corner.

She was down too, walloped by a blow, by some man, and she thought, I understand. She thought, This is easy. She thought, It's as easy as my first fuck. She had opened up so wide.

In the street, crossing to go home, her purse swung on her arm by its strap. She thought the dark air was so soft to walk through.

And for all that the girl knew there had not been a jot on her when she looked—no proof JACK WAS HERE! on her skin in red and in bright green ink, with any exclamation she could see, about them doing things, or about any one of them being of the opinion that her tits sucked.

And for the rest of her life, the girl, the woman, she never made a mark on anyone either that proved anything absolutely for certain, that she could ever see, about what she had done at any time, and this does not break her heart.

Forty Thousand Dollars

When she said forty thousand dollars for her diamond ring, where did I go with this fact? I followed right along with her, hoping, hoping for a ring like hers for myself, because of what I believe deep down, that she is so safe because she has her ring, that she is as safe as her ring is big—and so is her entire family—her husband who gave her the ring, all of her children—and no one has ever tried to talk me out of believing this fact, because I would never speak of it, that the entire quality of her life is totally secure because of the size of that ring—that the ring is a complete uplift—that every single thing else about her is up to the standard the size of her ring sets, such as even her denim espadrilles, which I love, which she was wearing the day she was talking to me, or her gray hair pulled back, so serene, so that she is adored, so that she is everlastingly loved by her husband, and why not?—just look at her!—and she is loved by her children, and by everyone like me who has ever laid eyes on her and her ring.

She was waggling it, which I loved her to do, because I loved to see it move, to see it do anything at all, and she said, "I make my meat loaf with it." She said, "I like that about it, too," and I saw the red meat smears she was talking about, smearing up the ring the way they would do, the bread all swollen up all over it, all over the ring part and the jewel. I saw my whole recipe on that ring.

She said, "It goes along with me to take out my garbage, and I like that," and I saw what she meant, how it would take out the garbage if it were taking it out with me, how it would go down with me, down the steps and out the back door—the ring part of the ring buried in the paper of the bag—and the dumping we would do together of the bag into the sunken can, before the likelihood of a break or a tear, or maybe I'd have to step on top of a whole heap of bags that was already down in there and then stamp on the top of the heap myself, to get it all deep down, to get the lid on with the ring on.

She said, "I never knew I was going to get anything like it. All that Harry said was, 'We'll need a wheelbarrow for you *and* the ring when you get it.' A wheelbarrow!" she said. "But now don't worry," she said to me. "You'll get one someday, too. Somebody will die," she said, "then you'll get yours—" Which is exactly what happened—I never had to pay money for mine, and mine ended up to be even bigger than hers. "This much bigger—" I showed her with two fingers that I almost put together, the amount, which is probably at least another carat more, but mine is stuck inside an old setting and cannot be measured. That was the day I walked behind her, that I showed her, that I walked with her to her car when she was leaving my house.

The rings were of no account outside, when we were saying goodbye, when we were outside my house going toward the back side of her car, because we were not looking at the rings then. The heels of her denim espadrilles, which matched her long, swinging skirt, were going up and down, so was her strong ponytail, and her shoulders, and I wanted to go along with her to wherever she was going.

And then the sense I had of not being able to stay behind her—of not being able to see myself in my own clothes walking away—the sense I had that I was not where I was, that I could not possibly follow in my own footsteps, was gone.

Pornography

I just had a terrible experience—I'm sorry. I was yelling at my boy, "Don't you ever!" I saw this crash. I saw this little old man. The door of the car opened and I saw this little old man tottering out. Somebody said, "I saw him!" The same somebody said, "He's already hit two cars."

There was this kid. He wasn't a kid. He was about nineteen. He was screaming and screaming on a bicycle.

Then I saw him, the kid, on the stretcher.

That little old man did more for me than any sex has ever done for me. I got these shudders.

The same thing with another kid—this one tiny, the

same thing, on a stretcher, absolutely quiet in a playground, and I was far enough away so that I did not know what had happened. I never found out. Same thing, shudders that I tried to make last, because I thought it would be wonderful if they would last for at least the four blocks it took me to get home and they were lasting and then I saw two more boys on their bicycles looking to get hit, not with any menace like they wanted to *do* anything to me, because I wasn't even over the white crossing line, not yet, and the only reason I saw either one of them was because I was ready to turn and I was looking at the script unlit yellow neon *l* on the cleaner's marquee which was kitty-corner to me, when just off that *l* I saw the red and the orange and my driver's leg struck up and down hard on the brake without my thinking, even though I think I was ready to go full out at that time, because where was I going, anyway? back home to my boy?

My car was rocking, the nose of it, against the T-shirts of those boys, first the red one, and then the orange one, and they each of them, they looked me in the eye.

Back home, my boy, he's only five, he's going to show me, making himself into a bicycle streak down our drive, heading, he says, for my mother's house, heading for that dangerous curve where so many horrible accidents have happened or have almost happened. What I did was yell at him DON'T YOU DO THAT! but he was already off, and then this goddamn little thing, this animal, this tiny chipmunk thing races with all its stripes right up at me, but not all the way *to* me, and then the thing, it whips around and runs away, like right now with my boy—I can't—there is no other way to put it—I *can't come.*

Here's Another Ending

This time my story has a foregone conclusion.

It is true also.

After I tell the story, I say, "You could start a religion based on a story like that—couldn't you?"

The story begins with my idea of a huge dog—a Doberman—which is to me an emblem—cruel, not lovable.

The dog is a household pet in a neighborhood such as mine, with houses with backyards which abut.

The huge dog is out and about when it should not be. It should never be.

When the dog returns to its owners, it is carrying in its

mouth a dirty dead rabbit.

The dog's owners exclaim—one of them does—"The neighbor's rabbit! He's killed it!" The dog's owners conclude, "We must save our dog's reputation at all costs." They think, Our dog is in jeopardy.

The dog's owners shampoo the dead rabbit and dry it with a hair dryer. At night, they sneak the rabbit back into their neighbor's yard, into its cage.

The morning of the following day, the dog's owners hear a shriek from the rabbit owners' yard. They think, Oh! The dead rabbit has been discovered! They rush to see what's what.

One of the rabbit's owners—the father in the family—is holding the limp, white rabbit up in the air. He says to the dog's owners, "We buried her two days ago!"

The dog's owners explain nothing. They won't, but not because they are ashamed of themselves.

There is another, more obvious reason.

Glass of Fashion

My mother touched the doctor's hair—"Your hair—" she said. I was looking at the doctor's eyes—black and as sad as any eyes I had ever looked at—doleful, mournful—but I thought she is hard-hearted too, this doctor. She must be hard-hearted. Hard-hearted is part of her job. It has to be.

The doctor's hair was full and long and kinky and wavy and black. My mother's hair is short and white and kinky and wavy and I could see why my mother was admiring the doctor's hair. I was admiring the doctor's body in her jeans. She had what I thought was a girlish and perfect form in her jeans, an enviable form.

There were four of us backed up to the large window at the end of the hall, because I had said, "Let's go over to the window to talk"—my mother, my sister, and me, and this very young woman doctor with black hair, black eyes, and jeans on.

We were at the window at the hospital, at the end of a hall, down from what was left of my father. We were getting the report on my father, because I had said to the doctor, "Tell us."

Maybe the doctor was a little ashamed too, or belligerent, when she was telling us. Her eyes had such a film over them, so that they sparkled when she spoke of his cerebellum, about his brain stem, about the size of his cortical function. She said, "He doesn't know who he is. He does not know who he once was. He does not feel grief or frustration. He does not know who you are." What I was envying then were the doctor's legs in her jeans. "Maybe—" I said, "you know, maybe—he had such a big brain before—it is just possible," I said, "that even if his brain has been ravaged, he is still a smart enough person."

The doctor did not say anything about that. No one did.

Chrissy, one of Dad's day-shift nurses, was coming along then toward us. Her glasses are the kind my sister will not wear. She will not get glasses like that. My mother will not either. A serious person's glasses—even if Chrissy is only just a nurse, even if she cannot explain very much about the brain, because she explained to me she has been out of school for too long—I can tell she is serious, that she is serious about me too. If she were a man, I would call what we have shared romantic love—we have shared so much, so often here—talking about my father with feeling. If she were a man—even if she couldn't remember half of what she had learned about the brain—even if she had forgotten it all—*no*—if she had forgotten it all, totally, I don't think I'd want to spend the time of day in her presence. She would disgust me if she were a man like that. So when she called us, when she said, "Your father—" and then when I called "Dad! Dad!" from the—and it sounded even to me as if I expected he would rise up—then I was ready for what I was feeling when I touched his forehead—which was still warm. His mouth was open. The front of the lower row of his teeth was showing. The teeth had never looked, each of them, so terribly small. Some of his teeth were the last things on my father that I ever touched.

Passage of the Soul

She said, "Don't get excited," to the scar-faced man.

He was excited, more like agitated. I remembered lots of men I have been with being like that. It was a worry. Maybe he was someone who shouldn't have been out.

She said, "We don't have to stay," and then I saw him in the snack line, way behind me, stuck in the heavy crowd, from where another woman's voice scolded somebody, "You had to pick the most popular picture of all the pictures!" Next, I found my husband. I always can. He goes ahead without me for the seats.

We hardly speak in theaters, waiting. I twisted myself

around to watch a girl behind us feed her boyfriend one popped kernel of corn, and then kiss him, and I saw him touch her breast, because we had to wait and wait, even for the previews to begin. I decided her boyfriend was no one I would want touching from, and I didn't flinch; he did, when I watched him watch me make my decision. It was as though he couldn't believe it, that he couldn't believe it—that I would judge him with such haste.

I would have run off with the character named Tom in the movie, so that they could see once and for all, as he put it to the woman, how they would be together, away from all of *this*. She ended up unappealing. She must have had a moment of horror—the actress—when she first saw herself like that.

At one time, seven years earlier in the movie, it seemed the whole audience had heaved a huge sigh watching her—not me, I just listened—I never would want to let on what I was thinking, You are so bold and lucky, when she dropped the prophylactics into her purse before she went out, and I was eager to see what would happen.

There are so many other things to recount about that movie. I left the theater with our balled-up empty popcorn bucket in my hand, to throw it away at home: that's what I was thinking about on the way to our car, that I'd have to hold it in my hand, which I did, feeling it, the squashed-up waxy rim of the bottom of it, all the way home; that somehow I had ended up like this. I had missed, just to begin with, the opportunity to throw it away inside the theater.

When we were getting ready for bed, I got myself into sort of a state. I saw that my husband was wearing what I considered to be the trousers of my pajamas—I have only one pair—which I had planned to put on, which had belonged to him once long ago, it's true, but hadn't he given them to me?

"What do you think you're doing?" I asked him. "I don't get it. What are you doing?"

I saw him, his body, his bare chest, which is sleek and perfectly formed by my standards—he was pulling down and folding the spread of our bed, in those cotton striped trousers. My husband is so graceful, how he moved around the foot of the bed was so graceful, how he gently, carefully folded.

Oh, he gave me back the trousers; so then we slept.

I didn't know what the issue was.

When the ringing of the telephone woke us in the night, we both knew what it could mean—everybody does—or it could have been just somebody borderline, wanting to hear the sound of anyone in a fright. That's what it was that time.

More will happen.

It will be stunning.

It's what I'm waiting for.

Some people are lucky—just walking, just going around, when you look at them.

Screaming

I thought she had grabbed her whole pearl necklace in a fist to stop it at her throat so that we could speak, because it had been crashing into itself, back and forth across her breast, as she was moving toward me.

"Your dog Heather"—was all I could think to say to her—"I still remember your story about Heather, your dog, and about your daughter coming down the stairs in the black wig."

"That was Heidi," she said.

"Your daughter is Heidi?"

"No," she said, "that's the dog."

"Oh, and she's not living," I said as she let the pearls go and they fell back down against her chest.

"That's right," she said. "Heather is. Heather's a better name—that's why you remember Heather. Heather is—" and she rolled her eyes so that I would know that I should have remembered Heather.

We did not talk about Heidi anymore that night, and I did not bring her up for conversation, because I did not have to. I spoke to her husband instead.

Still, I remembered how when the daughter was coming down the stairs in the black wig, wearing the kimono, Heidi ran away. I want to say that Heidi ran away screaming when she saw the daughter—but Heidi is the dog. She was a dog.

For the sake of conversation, when her husband and I saw a woman neither of us knew, I said, "I bet she's not afraid of a living soul." I said it because the woman had obviously done her hair all by herself for this gala—just stuck bobby pins you could see into her white hair, just worn an old, out-of-fashion cotton dress.

I told the husband I'd like to shake that woman's hand and ask her if it was true what I had guessed.

I was considering it, getting up close. I wondered would she get scared or what she would do—what I would do.

"What about that one there?" her husband asked.

That one there was a woman who was trying to get back behind my husband. The woman was wincing as if she had just done something awful.

"A gambling problem—that's what she has," I said. But that wasn't sordid enough. So then I said, "I don't have a clue."

"Now me," the husband said. "Do me."

"You," I said, "you are hardworking. You are—"

"No," he said, *not that*—" The man looked frightened. He looked ready to hear what I would say as if I really knew.

Then someone was at my back, tugging at my hair, moving it. I felt a mouth was on the nape of my neck. It was a kiss.

I did not have the faintest idea who would want to do that to me. There was not a soul.

When I saw him, when I turned, his head was still hung down low from kissing me. He was full of shame.

Thank God I did not know who he was.

I kept my face near his. I liked the look of him.

I was praying he would do something more to me.

Anything.

The Divine Right

"What your king did—" she was saying to the Dutchman.

"King? Do you even know the country? You don't even know which country. We have no king," the Dutchman said.

"No king? Your consort—the queen's consort?" she said.

"You mean the prince?"

"Bern—Bern—what he did was terrible, taking all that money. Why did he take the money? He doesn't need the money. He's married to the richest woman in the world."

The Dutchman laughed. "The richest woman in the world? Do you think so? Well, I hope so."

"Doesn't she own most of Fifth Avenue, along with that

other queen? the Queen of England?"

"Well, I don't know," the Dutchman said.

"You don't know? You don't think it was a bad thing what he did, taking that money?"

"No, none of us do," the Dutchman said. "We all like him very much. The money was offered, and he took it. It's no big deal."

"Well, here we all thought it was terrible. I thought it was. I hated him for it. I felt so sorry for the queen."

"What I can't get over," the Dutchman said, "in your country, are all those rich people's names plastered all over your museums—those plaques. Rich people in our country would never do that. They would be so embarrassed to do that."

"They would be?" she asked.

"Yes. They would never do that."

"Well, I wouldn't really do it either," she said. "Maybe a tiny tag that I had donated this or that, but not a huge plaque announcing a whole wing or anything like that. That would be embarrassing. It would be so obvious."

"What you were after?" the Dutchman laughed. "Are you very rich?"

"What?" she said.

"*You*, are you *rich*?" the Dutchman asked.

"I suppose that I am," Mrs. Osborne said. "Will you excuse me, please?"

In the mirror of her host's bathroom she saw her small oval face and her large earrings, each earring the size of one of her ears, rectangles of lapis lazuli framed in gold. She was embarrassed by the size of the earrings. She took the earrings off. She slipped them into her purse.

She was embarrassed by the size of her purse, the leather was too luxuriantly soft. She remembered the cost of the purse. She remembered the cost of the earrings.

She found Mr. Osborne in the host's kitchen, pouring himself a glass of wine. "I want to go home," she whispered.

"You tired?" Mr. Osborne asked.

"No," she answered, "I am not tired."

She held her gloved hands up in front of her as they walked to their car. She thought her gloves were a gaudy shade of green. She remembered the cost of the gloves. It would not bother her never to wear them again.

Sliding inside their car, she was afraid suddenly they were being watched. In this neighborhood, for the price of the car, they could be killed. They could be killed anywhere.

Mr. Osborne petted his wife's arm, before he turned the key to begin the drive home. He was petting the sleek seal fur of her coat. One of his hands, the glowing flesh of it, was all that she could see. She was frantic. She thought, What if I am really adored too—if it is true! She remembered.

Power

How do they do it? She cannot bend her legs.

Here I go, I must see him propping up her legs some way onto his shoulders, or with some contraption that they have had to devise, or do they simply put a bunch of something under her hips, or does he get into her from behind when they are lying down? or something else so obvious, but I don't know. She sits in his lap in a chair? and does it hurt her, because it is awkward? or do they even bother to try because it is never fun? Or does she do it for him some way with her mouth? How would she do it that way?

Her legs shine under the mesh nylon of her hose. I look

right at her legs when she says, "Oh, these legs." I do not know these people, the husband, and the wife, or the driver of this car that we are all paying to please get us home. At least, I know I have been away.

I do not know where to begin with this injury—with the sharpness of her nose which seems to solve something, the brightness of the light shooting off from her lacquered cane, or her laughing many more times than once, so that her husband said to her, "What is the matter?" or her ever-constant soft drawing up of a breath through her nose—once, then twice, and then pause—the sense of the stupid loss of time, that for once did not matter to me.

I thought, Let us keep on at this looking for the house they are looking for. It does not matter that the driver of the car cannot find it. Once I thought that.

She said to me, "I did not mean to throw my cane at you."

The door of the car had opened, the cane had been flung by someone onto the seat toward me, then her body. She had flung her body onto the back seat the wrong way—flat out and on her back—because of her problem, her big problem, her husband's bigger problem, their terrific problem.

She said, "No, this is not it," whenever the driver beamed a light on a house.

I said, "It is so dark." Finally, I said angrily, "Is this even the street?"

The driver said, "Yes!" and then I saw LOCUST in block black letters on a white sign on the corner at just that moment when the driver spoke.

She said, "No, this is not it."

When finally it was the house—those relatives, those people up there who came out onto that cement porch, who maybe call themselves friends, were not happy enough to receive their guests. That chirruping woman with her arms around the other woman didn't fool me. Nobody fooled me, but probably somebody was being fooled.

At least I knew where I lived. I could say to the driver, "Straight east now, and then left at the light." I could say it and say it and keep on with it, even with a righteous sense of anger—thank God—with a sense of—*You listen to me! This is how you get somewhere!*

But all this is not about failed love.

Somebody please tell me that this is all about something else entirely which is more important.

Somebody smarter and dearer than I, be the one available for my best, my most tenderest embrace when I have been convinced by you.

I could be a believer.

What Is It When God Speaks?

This was the house which once inspired a sister of one of the guests to declare, "People kill for this."

That's where the guests were on the perfect afternoon, not the sister.

It was a shame the afternoon became evening before the guests had to leave, not that anything was less lovely because it was evening.

There was a tender quality to the lack of light on the screened-in porch where they all were sitting, as there was also a tender quality to the small girl too old to be in the highchair, but she was not too large for it. The girl had insisted the highchair be carried out from the kitchen onto the porch. She had insisted on being put up into the highchair. She was ecstatic to be locked in behind the tray.

Her hands tapped and stroked the tray. She was not up there to eat. It was past time for that.

Behind the handsomest man on the porch was the array of green leafy trees and lawn, lit by a yard light, veiled by the black porch screen. The handsomest man smiled. He was serene.

Across from him, his wife, on the chintz-flowered sofa, who was the most beautiful woman, smiled serenely at her husband. She said of her husband to the others, "He never wants to leave here. Look at him! He likes it. The food is so good and healthy. He can keep swimming in your pool. Look at him. He is so happy!"

Then the man lifted up his girl, who was smaller than the other girl, who had never ever—his girl—been irritable even once, there at that house, and he put her up onto his shoulders. Her short legs were pressing on his chest, because he had wanted her legs to do that.

Her father felt his daughter on the back of him and on the front of him, on top of him, all at once. She was slightly over his head too, her head was. Her light heels were tapping lightly on his chest. He took her hands in his. She was ready for the dive that would not be possible unless he would fling her from him.

He should.

To Die

I undressed myself. I wanted sex—I wanted sex—I wanted sex—I wanted sex.

I climbed into bed with my wife.

She wanted sex with me. She always wants sex with me.

When I discharged myself this time into her, I was feeling myself banging as high up into her as I have ever gotten myself up into her.

I had just done the same with another woman who always wants sex with me, too.

There is another woman that I do the same with.

There is another woman.

There is another woman. There are five women who always want sex with me. They are always ready. It does not matter when or what or where, but they are ready.

I have a great deal of money which I have earned. I have physical beauty for a man. I have intelligence. I have work to do which I love to do, but women are what I prefer to anything, to lie down with them, the turning to touch the woman and knowing I will be received for sex as soon as I wish to be welcome.

I have been at it like this, this way for years. It does not matter when I will die. I have had everything I have ever wanted.

I should die now.

There should be a killing at my house.

There should be much, so much more for me, which I am not able to conceive of.

A Contribution to the Theory of Sex

Danny Ketchem had found himself compelled, or rather, *repelled* by his lack of understanding of what had become her whole life.

It is immaterial who *she* is. She could be his wife, his mother, his daughter, his best woman friend, these, or any combination of these, or add in any other female you can think of that she could be.

What the female's life had become is also immaterial, because Danny, in any event, was bound to get confused.

Her name is Nancy Drew. Real people do have her name.

Then Danny was towering, when Nancy held him, which was her idea, and his penis was sticking itself in between her breasts, as if a button were being pushed.

Remember, Danny could be a small-sized boy standing on a stool, getting hugged by Nancy, or a tall grown-up, not on a stool, and Nancy could be short.

Some time later, but not much later, Danny was on Nancy's lap. This could happen in all of the conceivable cases.

The object—Nancy's idea—was for her to wipe that grimace off his face.

Nancy cannot, she will not bear an ugly face. She tries not to—poor schmuck. She'll try anything. I know Nancy.

I want to wipe that grin off her face. It's so easy when you're one of us.

Marriage and the Family

Every time I go in there I am thinking, This time I will get the sisters straight, which one is which. But each time I go in there I think there is a new sister, one I have never seen before, who gets me mixed up. This new sister will act as though she knows me very well, as though I am quite familiar to her.

What is the same or almost the same about all of the sisters is this: their hair and their clothing, their faces, their jewelry, their ages, their expressions, their attitudes. I do not think they are quintuplets, if there are that many of them, or anything like that, but there is the possibility.

The sisters run a business where there are balloons around. It is a print and office supply shop in my town. It is new, and they behave as though they will be very successful, or as though they already are.

Everything is clean, such as stacks of tangerine and fuchsia paper for writing, and pens to match, which must be too expensive to buy. I wouldn't buy the pens.

Two or three of the sisters may be married. They wear tiny rectangular or round diamonds set into gold bands, and plain gold wedding bands to go with. A couple of the sisters only wear the diamonds.

There is a blond child I saw once, who looks happy and well adjusted. One of the sisters laughed and joked with the child. She hugged him and she kissed him.

A mother of a sister called in once, and she was spoken to sweetly by one of the sisters.

They do wear very tight pants. The pants hug and squeeze their bottoms so that there must be some discomfort for the sisters when they have to sit down to do their work, or even when they just stand—the pants are that tight.

I have never had an argument with one of the sisters. One of these sisters has never ridiculed me, or made me feel unwelcome, as though I were trying to take over in there, or take advantage of any of them, when I shopped there.

Not one of the sisters ever yelled at me, told me to get out of her way, or implied that I came into the shop too often, and that something was suspicious.

I never yelled back at one of the sisters to say I buy a lot in her shop, and that I could just go somewhere else. I never said I have my whole life in my hands when I come in there. I never got myself into a rage. I never looked at a sister and thought, You frighten me more than anyone I could ever look at—take a look at you—and your whole attitude is wrong.

Your attitude is abysmal. Your attitude is as if you have been stung, or are stinging, or are getting ready to be bitten, or to bite.

The last time I was in the shop, this is what happened: a man was in there. I didn't know for what purpose. He looked suspicious. He didn't buy anything. He was darting around, and he was looking at me, and looking at me, until I had to pay attention to him. Then he said, "I saw you out there," meaning out in front of the shop. What he meant was, he had seen the way I had parked my car. I knew that had to be it. I had even surprised myself with the way I had done it. I had never done anything like that parking.

I was proud of myself like a hero should be proud, who risks his life, or who doesn't risk his life, but who saves somebody, *anybody!*

"You could have killed somebody!" was what that man said to me.

Oh, My God, the Rapture!

The man was looking at the woman's breasts.

The woman thought, Oh, my God, I've forgotten myself, as she saw the man, another patient, at the end of the hall, looking at her, as she realized her paper robe was open, that she had left her paper robe open like that, while she was going as she had been directed to go into another room for the cardiogram. But since he had already seen her, there was no point, she thought, to closing the robe up.

"Go in there," the nurse had said. "That's right."

Lying down, waiting for the nurse, the woman looked at the tall window that rose at her feet which to her showed a very boring sight—some greenery and sky—and then the woman thought it would be so right to have a man who was not her husband make love to her. She thought it would be the rightest thing imaginable, and she was feeling what was to her the glow of perfect good health.

It was like hand lotion, the woman thought, that the nurse was putting on her breasts in small dabs. The woman didn't look—like white—she didn't look, lotion, and it was gooey and cool, not painful, very relaxing, the whole business.

"Now don't be alarmed," the woman told the nurse, "because my cardiogram is like the cardiogram of a sixty-year-old man who has just had an attack. Did the doctor tell you not to be alarmed?"

"No," the nurse said, "not for you he didn't."

"I'm just too small in there for my heart," the woman said. "It's being squeezed, so it looks funny, and it sounds funny, but I'm all right. It's all right."

There were short black wires that the woman thought the nurse was either untangling or rearranging in the air, and to her the nurse looked happy.

The woman wanted to make the nurse even happier by chatting with her, by making the nurse laugh. But the woman's mind came to a stop on it, on the thought of it, on the thought of wanting to make someone happy.

"Oh, my God," the woman said.

The nurse opened her mouth and smiled as if she might

be going to say something. She was operating the machine behind the woman's head which the woman thought was making a small unimportant noise. The whole business was so soothing, the whole cardiogram part. It was the easiest, the most relaxing thing, the woman thought.

When the doctor hung the woman's X rays up in front of her, the woman didn't even want to look.

When the doctor said, "You see, I think it's pancaked," when the doctor said, "I think it's because of your funnel chest," the woman said nothing.

"You know," the doctor said to the woman when the woman was leaving, "you ought to come in here more often."

The woman didn't have to pay the bill just then. The nurse said she did not have to, that it was not necessary, but the woman wanted to do it for the nurse.

So the woman said to the nurse, "I want to pay you now. This was wonderful. This never happens. You hardly kept me waiting at all. You took me—" she said, "you took me just when you said you would."

The Future of the Illusion

It was an intimate relation that we had had because hardly anyone else was listening in, except for a new employee who was learning the ropes.

The clerk looked at these beans, and she said, "Those are the ones I always use." And I said, "You do?"

Then she said, "Why don't you use the canned?"

That is the finale for that. That is the end of my retelling of it, because that is the end of what I view as the significant event. Everything else about the event withers away for the retelling except for the sight of the clerk's mouth.

Questions and answers: How did the clerk and I know

when enough talking was enough? I don't know. Did we care that we were deadly serious? I was surprised by it.

The clerk's upper lip is neatly scalloped. Together, her lips pout. They are the same to me as my childhood best friend's lips—the friend I had physical relations with, with a blanket over our laps on the sofa in my house.

We were girls side by side touching each other up in there where the form of the flesh is complicated. I do not know if I touched as well as she was touching me. We were about nine or we were ten, or we were eleven, or thirteen. I have no memory of sexual sensation, nor much of anything else.

I see us from the front because I am the person watching us, standing in front. I am the person who was not there at that time, who does not know whose idea it was to try, who does not know if she was the one who was afraid of being caught, if what she was doing was being done wrong.

I am still the odd man out, going backward for my training, for a feeling.

The odd woman, actually.

Boys!

It was as if I heard a hiss come out of my mother, or she was letting me have it some way with air when I said to her *You look so beautiful.*

But she didn't do that.

What she did do was she looked at me.

Maybe not even that, because I was standing—my mouth was at her ear—when I said You *look so beautiful,* so that no one else sitting at the table would hear. Was I whispering because her face had looked to me manhandled, if that were possible, with dips and curves lying pleasingly on her, pleasingly to me on her face?

So what happened then? Because it was *her* turn. Was I pulled away to say something to someone else?

No, I think I sat back down next to her. There was no getting away from her. I had been put there with her for the meal.

But I did not look at her. I was looking to see the shine on my plate rim, the sauce shine on my meal, and I was seeing the beauty of the man next to me, which was so careful in his hair, in his wife's hair that matched his hair, in his wife's pink mouth when she spoke. And with all this beauty going on, my knife, I kept it slicing competently through my meal. I kept it slicing, and I kept putting my knife back into the correct station on the rim of my plate after having sliced.

So when my meal was finished, and I felt that it was finished with no trouble, I got up and I left the people at the table. It must have been just for a moment when I got up, which was to go to the commotion why I finally got up, not to leave my mother—because I am a mother, too, and the commotion was my problem, my children, a disorganization.

My children were going around and around the table. I think that they were going so fast that I could not have caught the sleeve of even the youngest, even if I had tried reaching out for it. I think, maybe, I did try reaching out for it. But perhaps I didn't.

They all must have been waiting for me for what I would do, everyone else at the table—all the grown-up people—but

78

I was just looking at my children, my children going on and on, and their noise was like huge spills to me that kept being sudden and kept pouring.

And it was pleasing to me, *then it was*, in a certain way, the motion and the commotion, the children getting away from me, and I was watching it, and it was all my fault until the time when it would be over, and it wasn't as if anything could be ruined, I didn't think.

Then I called *Boys!* which I thought was loud, but when I hardly heard the word, because it was as if I had sent the word away, when the children hardly heard the word—they must not have—then I knew it must have been very faint out of my mouth, or just loud enough to be just another push of air to send them around again, to keep them going.

Then I saw a little girl, little enough that I must have missed her when she was going around with the boys, someone else's little girl, shorter than my littlest boy, that I did not know.

She must have thought she was so cute. The girl looked full of glee to me, and I was standing there, waiting for some other mother, the mother of the girl I did not know, to stand up and *do* something—because it was clear to me then that this little girl was the cause, that it was *all her fault*, and that she was the one in charge.

Ultimate Object

She did not know there would be a cupboard full of vases, but she had had a hunch, as when her tongue on someone's skin could give her a hunch of what would happen. Let me repeat—a tongue on someone's skin.

She was with a friend with whom she could share her joy that there was a cupboard full. She said, "We're OK! They've got everything we could ask for!"

She was crouched, flat-footed, her body nearly into a ball, except for her neck and for her head not conforming, so that she could look into the cupboard to let all the joy which was packed inside of the cupboard for her, into her.

One plastic vase with a bulb shape, with a narrow tube protruding from the bulb upward, was light as a feather, and was as warm as plastic is.

One glass vase, the shape of a torso, was covered all over with rough-grained glass, when she took it out.

She did not let her friend take vases away when she held up vases to prove they were unsuitable because she pronounced it was so.

Each time she went down, to look in, the quality of the joy was as good, did as much for her—four times.

It was festivity.

And to her, it was festivity, the cooking or the heating, that the man who had nothing to do with either her or her friend was doing nearby at the stove.

His peaceable plan—to lift and to unfurl, flat, round, yellow, black-speckled cakes—was the only other romantic transformation—not the product of imagination—going on in the place at the same time. And the man had no more right to be in this place—he was on the same shaky ground as she was, and as her friend was, by being there—which she saw him confirm with a smile.

It did not occur to her to get close to the man, to make an advance to taste, to do anything at all consequential vis-à-vis the man.

At the risk of startling readers, there was a dead body hidden not far from the man, which was the body of a woman the man had killed the day before, with a sharp enough knife, then lying—the knife was—in a drawer above the cupboard of vases.

The woman's naked, somewhat hacked body, decapitated and frozen, was in the institutional-sized freezer, adjacent to the stove. Out of her swollen face, her tongue protruded.

The wrong door, for all time, had been opened.

Again

Earlier, when my son was with me against his will, only for a moment, there had been a lot of baying we had heard on the radio. I had called to him, "Come hear the cattle!" but then thought, What a lie! when my son walked back out. Those had not been cattle.

On the radio—on the same program—I heard this woman saying she was better off. I was all by myself then.

She said the animals she ate were better off too. She said, "They're better off and so am I."

She said, "Most people think only of the chops and the steaks. They don't think about the ribs and the flanks and the neck."

She said, "I'll show you." She had some man there asking her questions. She said to him, "Let me show you." Then she was doing all this breathing, this gasping. She said, "God, I hate this. This happens to me every time." Then she said, "Come here, honey. Come here."

She was trying to get a lamb to come to her, I think. It was small, I imagined, like a baby lamb. She said, "Honey." She had to say it again. There was lots of wrestling that I heard.

She was wrestling with an animal which had ivory curls all over it, and gray, red-rimmed eyes, in my mind. She grabbed that baby lamb finally around the neck, her head on top of its head, I was thinking. She was hugging the baby, her pistol pressed into it somewhere, while the baby twisted to get loose, and she said, "Honey," again, and then there was this dull bang that I have heard, and the sound of falling down that I have heard.

It was at breakfast time when I heard the falling down, when I was caught next to the table I had set up for the breakfast. It was time for me to do what I do. I call.

The Nub

The cantor was slumped in the winged chair on the platform behind the pulpit for the time being.

I felt sorry for her, that we could not have given her applause for the job she had done. Something was definitely wrong when she was done, and we could not give her any applause, because she had sung her heart out.

That's what was wrong. I was thinking about the rabbi too. How could he know it right away that I thought he was boyish and candid, so adorable and appropriate for everything he had said to the thirteen-year-old girl on this great occasion?

He had stood with the girl in front of the open ark with his hands on her. I have never seen this. He was staring into her eyes. She was staring into his eyes for how long? for how long?

A matron with a navy velvet hat on, cocked saucily, began to weep when it was her turn at the pulpit, when she said the girl's name.

Then all of that was behind us.

Then to kick off the snowball dance at the luncheon party afterward, thirteen-year-old girls asked grown men, most of whom they did not know, to dance with them, on the order of the bandleader. Dessert—a sugary baked apple with cream—was served ahead of the main course, and then there was another dessert.

I was saying all of the appropriate things to everyone to get happiness from the happiness, to have a good time at the good time and I was getting it done.

Then, with the band, the thirteen-year-old girl was singing "I'll cry if I want to," and the bandleader told her she had done a good job when she was done, and we all gave her a lot of applause.

Later, at home, on the telephone, talking to my husband, only about this and about that, when I was in the same room with my children, I was pressing the nub of myself for the pleasure of the pleasure of it—my—what I am calling the nub—call it what you like—it was at exactly the point of the corner of my bureau top. I was pressing on this nub to get aware of the possibility of the pleasure, up and down. Then I did these very gentle moves over to the side of my nub on it, while I was talking.

What I was doing to myself, just so, was working for me, but nobody could appreciate what it meant to me, except for me.

A child learns from this. Children can learn all by themselves, if they have to, not to show off.

Mystery of the Universe

The five-year-old sitting at the head of the table said, *"Think!* You're not thinking. *Think!"*

So I tried to think, because he had said I had to.

"It has something to do with the angel," he said.

We all looked up at the lit-up Christmas tree, to the top, where I saw it pressed into the wooden beam, something golden and bent. The question, the child's question, was "What made the roof cave in?"

"He changes the rules when you start to guess it," his ten-year-old brother said.

It was true. I remembered his first hint—"It has something

to do with the train," which was on tracks at the base of the tree.

The size of the child's forehead, of his whole head, is astonishing for anyone of that age, for a child of any age, for any person—the breadth and the depth and the length of it—and then at dinner it was full of the question.

"You're not thinking!" he said again. *"Think!"* when I said that the top of the tree had pushed through the ceiling, had made the ceiling cave in, and I am forty-two.

"No!" he said. *"That's not it!* Who can guess it what it is?"

There were two families together, guessing while we were eating. He wasn't my child with this question, but I wished that he were. He is a child to be proud of, who would force us to think, who would not let up. I didn't mind that he'd stoop to being sneaky. I was proud of him. I am proud of anyone who stands up to everyone, who would say it to everyone in front of everyone *"You're the kind of person who would pull out a tree out of our front yard and throw it down on the house!"* I was so proud of a person who would think of doing the scariest thing he could think of, and he isn't even Jewish.

Egg

She had never allowed any egg of hers to get into such a condition, looking unlike itself and bulging, which was why the egg had all her attention from where it was in the depth of the sink, and from the depth of where it had been all dark yellow in the bowl, which had not been very far down inside the bowl, for there was no depth of anything inside the bowl, no particular depths of anything in either of her kitchen sinks either.

When she walked off from the sinks, thinking of the egg—How unlike itself!—she heard a yell which was noise produced by standing water which was falling suddenly down deeply into the pipes below the sinks.

Variously, this yell was a choke to her, a slap, or the end of a life, so that she stopped when she heard the yell with her back to the sinks. She had the impression of a preamble.

This is the beginning of something.

She went and got another bad egg and gave it to the dog to eat out of the bowl, so that the bowl was scoured and banged about.

The dog, she thinks, gets everything, she was thinking later, walking the dog. He gets it, but pisses it and craps it away—daily—everything, and yet everyone shows the dog all of their love.

Even she loves and she loves and she loves the dog.

The dog goes along down the street and the people say to her, "What a nice dog," and "That's a nice-looking dog you've got there!" The dog takes her farther down the street than she intended to go, where then she is murdered.

The murderer loves and he loves the woman's dog for the rest of the dog's life. The dog loves the murderer in return. The love that they share is perfect. It is not a love that would stoop to being sexual.

Science and Sin or Love and Understanding

I am not going to look it up in a book or do research. There are those of you who probably know why the small switching tail of a small animal makes me remember how I want to copy lewd people.

If the answer to the question is: Animals set an example for people, then I accept the answer. Do I have a choice?

I gave my husband no choice.

The last time I shoved something down my husband's throat was when I cheated on him. Now I say to him, "I didn't want to shove anything down your throat."

"It's because I love you," was the puny thing to say. It

was puny compared to the size of the power which had made me say it to him.

The power had made me see things too. The power had turned him into the shape of a man wearing his clothes so he could leave me in the dark, standing beside his side of it, our bed. I knew I was seeing things.

He said, "I hear you."

I may or I may not cheat on him again. But the last time, I was standing up when I knew I was going to do it. I see myself on the street, deciding. I am holding onto something. Now I cannot see what it is. This is no close-up view. I am a stick figure.

I am the size of a pin.

*Some Sexual Success Stories Plus
Other Stories in Which God Might
Choose to Appear*

The Limits of the World

My adventures have led me to believe that I possess two powerful powders—genuine powders. The "I command my man" powder is one of my powders. When I put this powder on my body, then I will command my man. He will always be my lover whether he wants to be my lover or not. He will be obedient and satisfied, whether that's what I want him to be or not. Nothing will ever take him away, whether that's what I want or not.

I'm not sure what the purpose is of my other genuine powder.

Now what?

What would you do? Would you go ahead and use either of these powders, if you, as I have done, had gone ahead and paid money for them?

Keep in mind, we are past the age of enlightenment. This is past reason. We are pretty deep into modern history and the decline of religion. This is when Nature itself has been stripped bare of its cozy personality and we all feel homeless in our own natures as well.

To say it another way, I gave away a pure love powder with no conditions on its use, or specifications warranted. (A lusty friend of mine grabbed it out of my hand.)

So now what?

Whosoever reads this, write to me if I am still alive, or please write to my children, or to my children's children, who may yet be even still deeper into the farther reaches of our common history. Give us *your* opinion. Provide please credentials for you yourself, who you are doing the talking.

Are you a superior person? Or, how soon do you think you will be? I can ask because I asked.

My Highest Mental Achievement

Baby, I will miss you with your common sense, and with your blindness to psychology. My prediction for you is that you will have a fascinating life and that you will stay eternally young, and that you will never lack for love. I am interested in all aspects of you.

If I could know what happened the last time you had sexual intercourse with me, and what your opinion of it was, what your experience was with it, I would be so interested to hear. Could you tell me how this time this sin was different?

The last time for me, when I saw my own hair there beneath my swollen belly, the sight of my hair offended me. I would rather see how I pinned your legs. I had opened my legs for you, and with my saying "This is better for me," I had twisted around onto my side for your sexy behavior. The big baby which was inside me took a beating. In any event, I do believe that sex, or even love, is not inappropriate for the very, very immature.

It is so much better for me to be the one who loves rather than to be the one who gets loved! It is so much better for me not to be the one who can take it or leave it—as you take it. Just think!—I actually became radical at the Grand Canyon when I looked around us and just kept my mouth shut there. It was the full scope of my achievement that I wanted to take a running start and then leap in. Don't forget, I like a mess!

Clean

This begins where so many others have ended, where the man and his wife are going to live the rest of their entire lives in perfect joy, so they arrive at the train station.

Now we're on our way. I'm dooteedooteedoing as if I'm happy. Went to the mail where I go to get it. Touched it. Washed myself. Meticulously washed out my contraceptive device with Cascade or Joy.

I toasted a piece of toast for myself to eat, buttered it, put cheese on it, drank coffee I had made, orange juice I had squeezed, took care of the other people. Put away food. I washed. I washed. I never thought I'd get the semen off my ring. The speed of my thought was a deep offense to me. It should have taken me a lifetime to find out how not to be happy just to ensure perfect success.

The Good Man

He called it a triumph that he never controlled her passions. That gadget with propellers, with the pads on the propellers, that he had used to produce ultra-pleasure for Darlene—his dream come true—was swell.

He was consoled by this ultra-pleasure briefly. Soon afterward, he died. He was alone when he died, because his pleasure-loving daughter had gone off to the theater.

As a dead man, prone upon his bed, this gadgeteer would be an inspiration either for Darlene or for his daughter.

One day, when he had been alive, so to speak, he had killed a hornet by slugging it, and then, before he realized what he was doing—seizing for himself an opportunity—he had consumed all of the fresh greens which he had heaped up on his platter, plus the strips of the boiled meat. That should have been the test of his manhood, because he is a darling.

Pussy

The woman's knowledge gives her vicious pleasure. She could have understood sooner if she had only tried to understand. Now that she understands, she will just not leave the men alone, now that she understands that everything that matters has nothing to do with her expectation of loyalty and devotion from a person she is hoping is nearly perfect. Oh yes, now the woman is full of desire as she climbs the stairs to her room. The stairs glow for her eyes. The woman sees a man heads taller than she is jump out at her and then turn back away. He is subtracting things from himself, because she can see only his trouser leg and his one shoe as he goes into her room.

Upon her entering her room after him, the woman does something significant and full of meaning.

Albeit, the orange orange, the thin, dry, oval slice of gray bread—oh no, there was even something more concealed in some silver foil—the elixir the woman knows emanates from these hors d'oeuvres which are all hers, on her tray, on the table, at the end of her bed—amounts to what the woman is if I say so. She equals anything at all on my say-so. The woman is a little dirty thrill.

This is the haunting story of a young man who married for love and who found himself in the grip of a considerable poonac.

Turning

We kept on and I did not break into tears. Meanwhile, I am wondering which one of us is the cruelest. I can hear my voice saying all of those things.

A few months later, he reminded me that our misfortunes were almost identical, because, he said, we had become inextricably commingled. When he said what amounted to that, I put my arms around him and I kissed him. However, my suspicion is that he cannot tolerate being confined by a woman.

When daylight came, we made our preparations for the day, by bathing, by dressing, by eating. My own appearance was of concern to me, but there was also my great suspicion about what we had been doing throughout the night. Had we succeeded? Should we have been rejoicing? controlling our anger? openly admitting where the true superiority resides? Or should we have kept on with our spirit of rivalry?

Anyway, I spoke seriously with him about my violent disposition. But just around the corner, I did not know what it was.

No sooner had the summer arrived—it was a day like today—with the sea whipped up by the wind, the sky was filled with action—with tumbling clouds, carrying on how they do, erratic, totally unstable, disorderly, maltreating each other's lifeless bodies, fabricating, evaporating ominously. I trust the unknown. I could never be astonished by such painless deaths apart from one episode, wherein I attempted to twist my fate, and to rear a child, among other things.

The Dog

She had every reason to think that he had had a good time with her when he licked thoroughly with his strong tongue the private parts of her body. She was in bed when he did this. He was her best friend.

When she awoke the next morning, she smelled the sweet lilac and the roses in her garden—she was aware of the thump of his tail—and felt a breeze spring in through the window screen.

She ate a small piece of fish for her breakfast. She hummed a little tune to herself—and when she opened a drawer, she observed an old crumb from some food in there and she thought, This is unbelievable.

Her husband, Frank, came in for his breakfast. Frank is clever, of course.

She said to Frank, "*Sit!*"

Really, she did not understand at that time why Frank didn't.

The Man

It was the best week of his life. I wasn't there for much of it. He used to try to copulate with my boyfriends when they'd come to the house and he'd chase around and chase around. He'd come when I called his name, and I would go wild screaming his name until he came running to me faster than I could ever run, so I'd sink to my knees sometimes to get down on his level with him, with his excitement, which was often running rampant. His bed was filthy where he rested and slept. He ate with gusto, made a great noise, and drank what he drank with a power to drink I will not ever forget. He influenced me a lot.

Really, Really, Really

Several times while she was wishing, she had looked out over a large body of water. For heaven's sake, she thought she could at least indulge her desire to see something exceptional a couple of times.

She bought a present for herself which she didn't think was good enough, at a huge personal cost, which was too high.

She's never really, really, really wished enough for anything in her life, or for a person, but she had thought she should indulge herself somewhat, so she sort of did. She kept indulging herself somewhat, until she went broke. Her goodwill toward herself was worthy of a king's or of a what?

The next year, when she visited France with her cousins Tanya, Luisa, and Margo, she went to the market a couple of times. Tanya chided her for being withdrawn. Luisa tried to cheer her up. Margo was indifferent to her.

When she was put into confinement, her hands and her feet were tied, her nose was clamped, and she was force-fed. Once more, a couple of times, she wished she could be a good person and that she would have the wisdom to make safe and sound decisions. This time this little bit of wishing made it so! *And I mean it!*

The Courage of a Woman

I am pretty sure that everything in our hearts is wise and pure and chaste.

He appreciates me. He admires me. Maybe he even worships me. Well, I worship him and everything he stands for, such as beauty, valor, intelligence, diligence, gracefulness, loyalty—I don't know if he cracks jokes, but there *is* such a thing as perfection!

We are very ambitious. We achieve everything a family should achieve—as much as we know about the goals of a family, what the goals ought to be. We cannot take ourselves too seriously.

After learning absolutely everything, we could not make mistakes. We could not make fools of ourselves. I have heard that that is dangerous.

I stay there most nights in our bed, in our bedroom. I do not get up off the bed once I get down into it. I am still talking with excitement about this fact, and marveling, how I find myself at the end of an hour still tireless and still safe. We have treasures and luxury. I have just bought for myself a pair of the most compelling earrings with little diamonds. People look at your ears before they look at your hands to see your rings. People may never look at your rings. Marilyn told me that. Marilyn hobnobs with duchesses and dukes and lords and all the nobility. Her life is just . . . it is very similar to mine if I knew more about her.

Marilyn's increasing popularity and reputation have given her personal stature, which I crave. However, in the spring of this year, there has been a distinct turning point in my life. We have just finished building our Sea Forest home and now we are not spending our money as usual. I keep myself hungry, so that I will shed some weight, so that when I look at myself, I am thinking to myself, I could just go ahead and fly.

I was walking humbly down the stone steps toward the sea with my husband, Frank, and with my son Ephraim. Ephraim was weeping.

"What is it?" Frank asked his son.

We had just, I had thought, all of us, been feeling nearly blissful, sitting together on our garden terrace.

I had thought Ephraim was blooming.

When Ephraim spoke, we watched him closely.

"What's the trouble?" Frank said.

For all intents and purposes, my mind is not keen.

The Circumcision

The infant is too young to hear the credo he should live by: *He should marry and do good deeds.*

I want to know what is going to happen—you know—will he end up being one of those people? I am one of those people—leading my life. Almost daily, my life is ideal for a person gifted with power and reason.

That the infant was substantially drugged was a good deed. I left without paying any respect, or without saying anything to the infant, because *who is it?*

Walking to my car, I see the other cars available to other people. I put my key into the lock of my car, but my key doesn't fit the lock. I am going to have to stick my key into another one. This is being repeated and repeated and repeated all over the world with impatience or maturity or dead to the world. The ease with which my key finally does do the trick puts a knot in my throat. I am a sad woman. My face is hard. My car is enormous. The road is an outrage that I follow with a blood lust to get to my home to my husband.

Whom I uncritically love.

Spanish

I wish that everything is enough for Mr. Red who is the husband, who has a heavy Spanish accent. He is a scholar. Mrs. Red speaks English with a heavy Spanish accent also, and she is a full-time scholar, too.

Yesterday, I saw the Reds' bed of scarlet impatiens waving in the wind, which was quite unremarkable. But, that is not all.

Mrs. Red, who is probably responsible for the planting of the flowers, was on her way, carrying her folded-up folding chair and several other things.

She was big enough, even with carrying all of her things, so she could fit comfortably between my thumb and my forefinger from where I sat inside of my house watching her—that was my perspective on my hand.

To me, she is like a cutie-pie! like a little doll!

Society, schools, hospitals, factories, and homes are the other victims of the perpetual movement of philosophical thought, as well as many other organees.

A Field That Can Never Be Exhausted

I must let you know how urgent I felt racing down the stairs. We did that—the whole group of us girls. Next winter I am going to be in Florida.

I didn't have any money with me. There was an additional obstacle. Things were probably not that simple. He said, "Follow the good-looking blond!" He was the blond he was referring to, and he was very good-looking, and jaunty, I thought. It was a cute idea to tell us to follow him and to use a line like that. He was having fun I think. Off we trooped. He shouted, "Single file!"

I suppose he had to shout that. I suppose there was no

other way to do it.

What do you expect? Don't you expect him to get a little fun out of his job? When he was telling me to pull my pants down, he said, "Pull them down lower."

But how should I tell this? I have been waiting for years to tell this anecdote that any civilization would need to illustrate that there are people, you know, who are perfectly capable of being cheerful.

They Were Naked Again

In an instant she may not see it as it happens, how light crowds in and around her red hair, and all around her head, before vanishing into some other light, which is likely having nothing more to do with her hair?—but this is wrong, because there is no inkling of science.

So—I'll get her into his bed, looking at his carpet, which is on his floor, rolled up. Together, they look at it, not for any reason they guess might augment them.

He is prepared to get rid of the carpet. It has been causing him to feel bereft of something he probably never had—something which I could give him.

I could.

She says, "Please don't get rid of it. It comforts me."

I would never say that to him. I would never say that to him in this situation, which is a situation which is a spectacular opportunity for them both, and it is my time they are taking.

You know what happens when they both are thinking so much about the carpet at the same time?

His experience appears to be one of elation, such as finishing. Then she says something obscene, which happens to be clairvoyant. Then I say, "I gave my own carpet away like that, *bitch!*"

But they cannot hear me.

I'll threaten suicide!

You—you think about a carpet.

Me.

The Meaning of Life

One point must be made and this concerns what we learn from the history of the world. It must be noted that usually men do not possess valuables or huge sums of money. Their sense of their being sorry about this grows and it grows and it grows. A woman may be their only irreplaceable object. That's why I think the meaning of life is so wonderful. It has helped millions of men and women to achieve vastly rich and productive lives.

Recently, this woman appeared on TV. She has a small head, a big head of hair, and she sings solo. She's wonderful, but because of her dread fear of almost all men, she does not want any more than one man at a time in her life, which is reasonable, but she is always at a loss.

The Hag Was Transformed by Love

The guys, oh, how you longed for them, round and savory, and just how they get after a few days in their gravy, in the pot, in the refrigerator, and then they are heated up, and then they are eaten up.

I know what Terri Great thought because I remember my thoughts to a tee exactly about my own little new potatoes I just ate, and I am calling myself for the hell of it, *Terri!*

She was sticking her fork—Mrs. Alexander Great—into the little new potato, thinking, I may be the only one who likes this!

For the hell of it, Mrs. Great, you should have stayed

there sticking in your fork, tasting and enjoying, and eating up little new potatoes until you had finished all four of your potatoes, *Terri!*

Say it, Terri, from the two and a half little guys that you did eat, you got all the stimulation from the spree you thought was wise, because, if she's going to say, "This is the best it gets from a potato," then Terri Great has stretched her mind beyond the wisecrack fully—stop!

Terri left the house then, and her husband Alexander never saw her again, nor her little guy Raymond, nor her little guy, Guy.

She spent most of her time in the company of people like herself who said they knew what they were thinking. For instance, *she* thinks any penis is ugly.

The enormity of what she had done, leaving her family abruptly, suddenly, and with no warning, gave her lots of other thoughts, too.

She did not upon arrival, speak well the language of the country she had fled to. When she asked a man, for example, on the street, her first day in town, "Where is the train station?" the man told her kindly that there had not been a war in his country for forty years. (He wore a brown, ankle-length, belted trench coat, was about sixty years old.) Miraculously, she thought she could comprehend every word that he had said. It was a miracle, too, that when he flashed it at her, she thought *his* penis was a beauty. Like magic—the colors of it were the colors to her of her own baby's shirt, face, and hat that she had only just left far behind, and the form of it was like a much much much bigger dewdrop.

At home, this rich man had a thin wife. He supposedly worshipped his old wife until old Terri Great came into the picture. Then just forget it. (Things keep happening so perversely for zealots.)

For Terri, she got her first six orgasms during penetration with this man during the next fifteen weeks of their intercourses together.

In the weeks that followed these events, she renewed her days, and she became intrigued with finance.

The Mistake

Stupid of me, but I am terrified. She is looking at me curiously. The natural thing is to act sympathetic to her, so I go ahead and do that.

Meanwhile, down the hall, a girl is getting angry. I can hear the telltale sounds. This girl comes in to say something.

Stupid of me, but I am terrified. The natural thing is to act sympathetic to her. She is looking at me curiously.

I don't know which horrible thing happens next in my real bedroom. The new carpeting is familiar. I know the bedspread. I know the room well, but I don't remember a clock around here that chimes. I remember mystery, suspense, and adventure.

Even as I blot it out, I was dead wrong to summarize.

Icky

Her curtains actually do stiffen and then billow into a deformity because of the warm gusts of wind which are periodic. The carnations in her vase tremble when it's their turn, which is poetic. In her beautiful room she is a bit ghoulish even when she is still.

She is also youngish and balding.

She is so lucky because a picture painted by her son in her beautiful room is revolutionary in its scope, scale, and ambition. All of the knowledge her son will ever need to know about ghoulishness is in it.

The son is correct if he chooses to believe that his

mother is a ghoul.

He thinks her armchair is as comforting as nobody he has ever known. There are flowers he cannot identify, printed on the upholstery, but their type, he is well aware, is icky. In her beautiful room where he has gotten her riding crop wet, among other things, his mother has stuck his tiny last lost tooth, with glue, onto the frame of her mirror.

A sensational evening is ahead for the boy, even though he is not allowed to bring food or drink into any room outside of the kitchen.

His mother has just asked him to do a couple of odd jobs for money.

Ore

A generally reliable woman was pestering the seed—or is it called a pit?—that she had noticed was blotchy. The reliable woman at work in her kitchen observed privately to herself, for no reason she knew of, that the pit had been discolored by avocado-colored markings. The woman was using her fingers to wrench the pit out from the center of the ripe fruit. The pit was not coming along willingly.

No, this is not about childbirth.

The surprise is that anyone as reliable as she is had not had plenty of experience wrenching pits.

The pear's pit—this is an avocado pear pit—was not of a

like mind to hers—like, *What is the matter with you, pit?*

What is the matter with her very reliable husband, who could not extract this woman, his wife, from their home?

The wife had been making her husband miserable for years, being the unbudgeable type.

I'd say time for a change.

In their secret life, the husband and the wife then sought the usual marital excavations—their aim being to meet their troubles with equanimity.

For starters, they agreed. They agreed how excellent their sexual satisfactions together were, how much more reliably attainable these satisfactions were, more now than had ever been the case before, now that every other aspect of their life together, they admitted, was so unsatisfactory in such extreme.

No, no, no, no, no!

This discussion never occurred. The husband and the wife no longer had the means to conduct such a high-level discussion.

These people are annoying. You know how annoying? To me, as annoying as it was to see for myself last night at twilight one bright sparkling spot in the sky that did not move. It did not get bigger, or brighter, or smaller, or dimmer, and for all intents and purposes, it is stuck there.

As I am.

The Care of Myself

So why can't everything be perfect? God love him, he appealed to me. He had startled me into feeling an incredible amount of affection for a stranger—him. Still, I could have made mad passionate love to him, this inspector who rang my doorbell, who had dressed himself as a fireman.

"Do you have a wound? Is that a bandage on your head?" I asked him.

He tugged on the stretchy cloth which was not supposed to be hidden under his helmet. He said, "We all wear that."

The days and the years pass so swiftly.

Now, what I am doing for my wound is this: I stick any

old rag or balled-up old sock I can find as close to it as I can get. Belly-down on the floor, with my reading glasses on, I've also got some filler sticking almost into my asshole. With my bawdy book here to comfort me right in front of my nose—we are both, the book and I, products of a great civilization—I take the plunge. I am thrusting mightily, and sometimes I manage to get hurt again.

Crush

There was no Weinberg. The server barging into all that with his tray of only a few nuggets on a doily was peevish with his back arched, with his chin up. A primarily good woman was introducing Mrs. Williams and a Darnell Hyde. The woman showed me where her waist was and her curved legs were visible to me when she marched over to a dressed-up man to say his name.

The rest of this story is about my family's poignant meal in the elegant hotel dining room. Within striking distance, there is a celebrity who thinks she should be eating here. She is exquisite and brainy and delicately made, it appears—or she is fashioned to appear to be delicate. Her lacy necklace sparkles around her neck. Her lacy bracelet on her wrist sparkles. At her throat her skin is deadish white and, elsewhere, her hair is white. The rest of this story is about my wish to be her. Her escort should be ashamed of himself. His back was turned to me the whole time.

My mother loved the food. I loved mine. I was marginally disappointed in it. I escaped when I said I had to go to the bathroom, the same way I forgot with my hand on the handle of the fridge door why I had wanted to look inside. It is a great natural law, I think, but of what?

Diane, I was the first of us to swoon, entering the glass elevator, descending—my only purpose being to resemble a human being going down.

A Progress in Spirituality

We were in our own backyard, with everything that that could mean, portending. This could be important.

To taste his drink, to look into his eyes, to be shocked, to give my opinion, I had been up on my feet.

"I am shocked. It is so sweet," I said. I was.

He said, "It is."

I sat back down.

The wind took his paper cup, almost blew it away. He got it back. He put it down. He picked it up. No-handed, he bit the rim.

"It's no trouble," I said. "I'll take it inside and throw it away."

My guess is, it was my "trouble" or my "no" he heard, when he saw my shapely form as I turned with his paper cup.

Things got all knocked back—I don't have a clue how.

To have seen his face then—what's it called?—turgid with lust for me?—was a forgotten truth, and tonight I am destined to shoot the rival woman who tried to snatch him. I shoot her by shaking her hand.

When I take her hot hand in mine, we could be the rivals dipped in stone, in the antique story. There should be a story. I don't know the story. There may be a story of them getting a grip on each other forever.

What does that mean? Nobody gets killed. I'm stuck with her. He's stuck with me. All I remember is our kinship, which makes me sick. I have gone so very far to deny death.

It is already only a memory.

The Band-Aid and the Piece of Gum

There was the possibility up until five o'clock—then there was no more possibility. I expected to hear from Walter today. When I woke up, I was cheered by the thought that maybe today, *today* would be the most important day of my life. Today I ended up using the Band-Aid Walter had given me on my toe. He had thrust it into my hand. "Take it. You never know when you may need it." The piece of gum he had once given me I chewed today finally also. "Try it. You could learn something," is what he had said. Remember how I told you he grabbed me around the neck the last time I saw him? It was practically impossible to walk, which he was trying to do all at the same time, and trying to get me to walk along with him, too.

There was the possibility, perhaps, that we could both have toppled over onto his floor.

That's it. Usually they start where a person was born, then their parents, their parents' parents, where they were born, occupations, so that includes dates, names, locations, character traits of all the parties concerned, chronology, trauma, wishes, dreams, eccentricities, real speech, achievements, including struggle, the obstacles, someone's dementia, another chronic illness, a centrifugal drama, certainly all the deaths, photos, paintings if any—likenesses of many of the parties concerned, plus summary statements made periodically throughout to sum up the situation at any given time.

Torah

I carry this plate of triumph into the school building with my Saran Wrap all aflutter all over my iced cakes. I have iced my cakes because I think everyone nowadays has an expectation of icing on it from a cupcake, as I am sure I do, too.

The corn candies I pushed into the icing are the tough lumps, my vicious triples, my quadruples, the repetition of an idea an idea an idea an idea an idea. Are you keeping track of this as I did? This situation could be handled.

I took control of the situation when the official in the office did nothing when she saw me create a situation in her office. But I gave up control when this official declared that no man had ever hooked his fingers into her vagina and then keenly observed her face, or pleaded to go down on her, or pushed her against a wall into her own shadow and said, "We call this dry humping when we do it in school!"

As it turned out, for no good reason, I tested the woman sorely.

I was wicked.

Yet perfectly delightful when I was God.

Jeweling

In the deep dark recesses of her curse, there lay everything she had.

She was an expert diver, but this had nothing to do with
that. She opened her purse and she told her friend, "Look in
here."

He said, "What?" but he looked inside. He was used to
acceding to certain commands.

She was showing him what he had given to her, where
she had put his gift—how the thing was situated in the deep
dark recesses of her purse.

Someone thought the object he had given her was an

object beautiful to look at.

He had just given it to her, and that is where it had ended up being—for the time being.

He needed no special perspicacity to know that she meant, *See how it looks in here, your thing in mine.*

He is a friend in a clandestine, passionate arrangement.

He is mine.

It is my purse.

Now his gift is all mine, with its deep capacity for spectral light. It is as cold and as hard an object as is the love I receive from two men. It is so hard.

I believe in coincidence and providence.

I believe in these two men as I believe in my right hand and in my left hand equally, and in my two eyes, that they are equally mine, and in my ears, and in the two of everything for and on me.

Two created me thereof, in the beginning. Is it precious? It took two to make me what I am.

Sex Solves Problems

There is no going back, and no use insisting I have a bath to look forward to. Is four o'clock too late? Dinner, sure.

As I carried the baby off for her bath, I felt I was doing the right thing. It was what I had been asked to do, and I was trying to be helpful. The baby was naked as a baby, and she took up almost all of the sink, and she was slippery when wet, and not at all easy to hold on to, and I don't think I got much of the soap on her, and she kept shutting her head up into the faucet.

"I have an idea," I said. "You better go to bed."

It was the greatest stroke of luck. It was like putting the

baby away. I am not a fusser. It was like having any old thing for dinner and not giving a hoot. This is so basic.

The first person who decided a problem could be solved came up with the idea the same way I did.

We are easy lays, too.

Seraphim

I suppose that I do have places, a few places, left to wear my mustache to. I have worn it almost everywhere. Before we go, I put on my fur coat inside of my house simultaneous with my putting it on. My mustache is faint and spiky. My coat is thick and dark.

Going around town tends to be sad, like walking around behind a dog who won't go. You wear what you wear. Tonight we are going to the Fontana for pizza. There will be a TV on in there. There will be plastic chandeliers to simulate glass chandeliers. There will be simulated oil paintings on the wall to simulate the idea of things: a woman with a hat on, perhaps her skirt roughed up by the wind, her hand lifted to keep her bonnet on her head.

When the pizza comes, I put a fingertip into my plate to get a crumb stuck to it, then to lick the crumb off.

This is my gift to my children—whereas theirs to me is not to be nasty about having a mother with facial hair.

I am telling you, I never wear it anywhere near my perianal or my vaginal-lips locations. If it as much as touches my eyes, I wash them out with a solution. I promise you—*you are an angel!*—I keep it out of the reach of the children!

My Radiant Girl

I am not so sure there is a reason to tell this except for my wanting to say things about magic, about myth, about legend that might brighten up your day, if you believe in magic, myth, legend. It was Coleridge who said we might brighten up the day this way. Emerson might have said there are real nymphs in your city park, if you look. Oh I'm sure Cocteau and George Eliot had their opinions on nymphs. Let's say Edith Wharton's daughter had the last word. I'm adding, though. My nymph in Central Park I did not know was a nymph right off. I believe thoroughly in her now.

The nymphs don't have to be little. She was. She had

removed most of her clothing. Men watched. There she was, oiling herself—an unblemished beauty with her teacup breasts, with boy hips, covered by her sunning suit, which she had had concealed under the other clothes, a necklace rimming her neck, and yellow hair tied back.

She looked at nothing except to do the sunning—to take care of the oil, her skin, and how she should rise up, or she should lie down, or turn—she had to look. Two men next to me, whom I also earnestly watched, watched earnestly.

I'm a woman. You don't take that for granted, I suppose, or that I believe in ghosts just because I say, "See the nymph!"

As Yeats said, "There are no such things as ghosts. Ghosts, no! There are those mortals who are beautifully masquerading, and those of them who are carried off." Okay, as Yeats did not say.

Sometimes girls like her are gotten rid of in a not so gentle way. Socrates said of one, "A northern gust carried her over the neighboring rocks, because I said so." He said, "I was swollen with passion." Nietzsche said the people of the cities have the machine to get rid of them if they are annoying.

It was Captain Stewart who informed me that because I saw the girl, "You will rise to the summit of your power, then you will die a violent death." He said that. His records confirm this fact.

So far, I have told the truth. It was straight from my heart to say we would be killed.

Bloom

The ham, the sweet and the tender cookies, pecans—
heavily grooved the way they are—candies wrapped in green
foil, in red, or in any foil, are the custom, so is the attitude of
the little girl named Sandy.

A man and a woman, not married to each other, who had
just returned, they said, from a romantic holiday together in
Capri, took turns to speak to each other respectfully of their
spouses and I listened in. One attractive man was there. Well,
I like him.

I leaped to my feet to go over to the attractive man, and
Sandy followed me. Since then, many others have tried to

stick to me like glue.

Please believe me that there is no part of me which is sad, angry, or resentful when I remember suddenly leaping up that time, or many other times since this time or before. The cause of my serenity may be that I am not ashamed to just go through the motions of having naked power and ambition, as in fucking.

This burgeoning is gratifying.

The Strangest and Most Powerful

"Look we've been over this and over this."

I giggled. I began to blush. I stammered, "You—you—Dicky—I—"

It was all unnecessary because—*blaaruah!*—the doorbell rang. Behind the window adjacent to the door, I saw a face and a fist.

Where we all were, at my aunt and uncle's house, was a particularly lovely spot. A group of people not yet too terribly tired continued making comments while I sat in a trance. My uncle opened the door. I heard my uncle say, "No, I won't do that," then another man's voice, "Why not?" then my uncle,

"I am afraid," then the other one, "Poor girl, she's the kind who gets taken advantage of." "What on earth do you mean?" my uncle said.

A certain kind of shock had set in, which protected me. I thought of going home. Of course, I made no attempt to leave. I was puzzled, and as per usual I spoke up. I did not comprehend or enjoy what I said, despite all of my experience talking. Then I laughed, and turned away with embarrassment. The next thing I imagined myself being spoken to. My uncle was handing me a drink, and a big stranger, with a purple orchid in his buttonhole, with his hair combed down flat, stood beside my uncle, gaping at me.

Clinkety-clink! clinked the ice cubes in my drink. I spilled some of my drink, of course, on my sweater, when the apparition began a conversation, which constitutes our culture. It seemed so trivial, our culture.

Ha

"See if you can find a whistle, even a toy whistle, *any* whistle," she implored.

He knew he'd never find one in their town. When you know how it will turn out, you feel tired. So do I.

There ought to be a brilliant portrayal of the homecoming—the boy with what? or with the lack of what? the matriarch to be reckoned with.

An hour later, the boy returned with nothing to say.

After her hesitation, his mother asked, "So?"

He heard her clanking their plates.

But instead of answering his mother, the boy went back

out into the backyard.

Because the mother's confusion was even greater than her boy's, she said nothing more either. But oh, how she thought!

Oh, this is hopeless! she thought.

What would her boy's fate be? she wondered. Well, she decided, they need a victim. I need a victim. We all need a victim.

The boy's heart heaved. He thought he was confident of the future. His house had been through fire. Things needed doing.

As for his mother, her voice had positively no timbre. She barely got her words out. In real life, she was barely heard.

About other details—or more about the boy—I don't have any ambition for any more, except to observe that the boy squatted on his haunches in the flowers.

The mother remembered then—that, as a baby, he had looked a trace displeased to be born.

The Revision

You should not read this. It is too private. It is the most serious. It is even too serious for me. I should make something of this.

Here is the best part, when he said to me *come here*. That was the very best part of my life so far. In the doorway to his bathroom was where I was. It was where I was when I asked him, "Are you peeing?"

He said, "No, but now I am." He was seated to do the peeing, so it would not be any problem to do it, facing me. I didn't even hear it, the peeing, if he peed.

Well, why?—why can't all of it be dirty parts, every part

a dirty part, or quickly leading to another dirty part?—the part when he just put himself into my mouth?—or the part when he said *you looked*—I can't remember how he said I looked to him, with that part of him in my mouth, but he jiggled on my jaw. He said *open up* before he went ahead and he peed.

Oh! That's how babies could be made!

The Time of Harmony, or Crudité

I would say I was half the way through when I thought to myself: Be careful. Anyway, there were twenty of them, to begin with.

I cut every one in half.

There were six.

I cut one to pieces, wedge-shaped. I'd say there were nine wedges. This is the estimate, generally, I get from thinking back on it.

I cut slices from it.

I'd say there were six slices.

I sawed and I sawed back and forth.

I cut stalks. I made chips. There were about fifty more wedges. There were wheels. One wheel which I had produced took off, rolled along, and dropped. I made sticks and I made slivers. I made raggedy bunches, stalks, chunks.

The house was neat and clean as ever. I got a lot of things done. I fully enjoyed sex. It turned out I was very deep into being.

On so many occasions, what goes with what? I do not want to leave behind anything during the accumulation that I will have to grasp at one glance because it is not a piece of crap.

Beyond Principle

It predestined her to become a thinker, to become a woman in a storm center for many years to come, because she did no fornicating with any other. She never left him out of it, *never*, not before she met him or after she had met him.

Into her mind she liked to keep adding what she called "a little curve" or "a little fork" among the pathways. She was ready to change her mind. Original conclusions were not her aim. She preferred to lay claim to the obvious.

One time when her hands were on his naked flesh, he said, "I love it when you draw me in." Squeezing his rump, "Like this?" she said.

Doing her job, she thought, *Who says that men aren't soft?* and the one man became the multitude through the backward path that leads to satisfaction, toward the upshot of all far-fetched speculation and curiosity—which is an example for example of how she first thought her idea of giving herself a little pinch or little pushes, of getting her hand up in between her and him in the very middle of their act. Not seeking to interrupt, to fail shamefully, or to baby herself, she intended to be serious—not to goof up, not to fuck up. "You're going to have fun with it, I know," she said. She thought, *I want to know how this turns out.* She said, "Come in and show me." She wagged her finger.

She cut him out of her life.

Isn't she wonderful, if an assumption is permissible? It looks as if she ended those embarrassing situations at any cost.

Her terrible war gave rise to pathology of this kind, but her terrible war finally put an end to temptation. Now I could throw in something that's so sensual, that's full of an object.

165

Scratching the Head

We respect her from learning from her. Let us compile the factors of her failure, We could not find hereditary factors. We said, "Tell us about yourself."

At the zenith of her life, in her mid-forties, she changed. She met the man who awakened her oldest erotic feelings.

"What a nightmare!" she said. "Why can't it be over? When I touched his arm, my hand was on fire. When I am nowhere near him, there's a sledgehammering down here."

She gestured, not shyly toward her genitalia. She inquired, "I have never heard of that. Have you?"

Perhaps we should leave the question as it is.

She asked herself aloud, "Do I have the moral force to finish my life?"

Her *phleglomania* was the *phenomenomenom* that had set in. Her highest average speed of forty-five miles per hour she achieved in her automobile. Sometimes she briefly closed her eyes, she said, while driving, because, she said, "What could possibly happen?"

She had a regal calmness. That should sound familiar.

Her instincts for victory, her naturally fierce nature, the entire inheritance of her species, the will to seduce and ensnare, all her cruel powers were melted into a cordial, into a very old sweet, smile—but that's what's been said.

Let us endeavor to sum up. How much repetition does it take? A perseveration? Biological investigation is required to explain the impulses and their transformations—the chief traits of a person. It is easy to forget, not that we ever should, that everything in this world is an accident, including the origin of life itself, plus the accumulation of riches. We should show more respect for Nature, not less. An accident isn't necessarily ever over.

Idea

The sound our feet made when we walked across his floorboards was a rhythmic accompaniment to physical desire both of us could have thought to put a stop to. It did occur to me, just on principle, to end that noise.

When I took off my coat, he said my coat was gray. I said it was green. He said it was gray.

In the upstairs of his house, when I sat myself down to look around, I decided I liked everything I was looking at. There was nothing I did not approve of, or that I did not admire that I could see.

He said, "You make such fast moves," when he was kissing

me. Then he said, "The watch—you have to take off the watch." Into the palm of his hand I put my watch, my four hairpins, my necklace made of silver beads.

He said, "That! Put that in your purse. I don't like that!" when I took off my brassiere. It remained there, though, curled up on his wooden floor, curled awkwardly for a piece of clothing, not awkwardly if it had been something else perhaps, a creature.

He said, "Now," he said, "use both of your hands so that I will feel you are really with me." Or, I was the one who said that to him—that's right, because I knew he could do things he would never want me to do. Add to all of that another distinctive feature, an atmosphere of awe, and something else that could be wet and gleaming which would not ordinarily be symbolic.

It Becomes True

Someone said, "See!"

I saw the chimpanzee doing some of its typical twists and it was flourishing its tail par excellence up in a phony tree. We're all here for a party.

If I said I love this, then what would happen to me?

"I love this!"

Nowadays it comes to the surface. This is the zoo. I am at a party which will be of considerable benefit to the zoo.

And fortunately for me, I got myself squeezed up in the arms of a man.

A good ways away from the monkey, we were dancing in

a tent. There was not one whiff of the monkey. The man swept me off my feet. It was my privilege. He swung me around. For this, I will always, always be grateful to him. I love this! Also, he surreptitiously slipped his hands along my body, lightly, so I would not notice, out there in front of everyone, while we were dancing. I was so grateful. I loved that.

It was not crude to break away to eat our food, to stick our forks into it by the prevailing standard.

There was nothing crude about my breasts popping up, the tops of them, when I just sat—the corresponding evidence pretty much up for grabs.

When did it happen?

I looked in vain for just one member of my family, or the most prominent person in my world. I was so grateful.

Typically, we are left, so many times. I love that routine—the horns of my dilemma—when they try to drag me forcibly away.

Going Wild

It is a dirty lie that there were no promises at this event in any shape or form because there was food.

There was also a discussion concerning the intellect of children. There was a child sucking a green lollipop and being admired by an adult for being adorable while he was sucking, lying down.

Based on my intuition, my dead father would not have had fun at this event.

I had some fun while I stuffed myself to the gills with the food until I was uncomfortable and then I was no longer having fun.

I petted the head of a two-and-a-half-year-old boy and by doing that I encouraged him to try another stunt. I did not scare him into changing. I succeeded with him by petting him while he was doing something—anything—and then I was redirecting him gently toward something less appropriate for his age.

We all stopped what we were doing, even I had stopped my chewing, and we had orchestrated ourselves to stare as a group at one child who acted as if he knew he should be center stage. I could have asked myself, What does this child wish for more than anything in the whole world?

Maybe there is one correct answer!

The one person who was giving me the most attention at the event is gone! evaporated right out of my sight! He's off into the pure air of my imagination where I imagine him with me lying down in a bed, where we discuss by what method everything is ordered.

Has there been one grand enough moment of either sex, or serenity, of soothsaying, or of silliness at the tragedy, during which time we paid homage to one object, or to a notion, or to one of us?

Thanks for letting, letting me even address you.

Satisfied is what I am.

Coronation

A royal person, wearing a royal robe, with something royal on his head—something exciting—there are other smudges, other noble people with him, fine furnishings, and precious objects, and so on. From where I sit on my toilet, the chrome soap holder, built into the wall, is looking great.

This magic makes me wonder. The concaveness is going convexly. It is a grand, miniature, several-storied window to look through, or a glass revolving door.

My *New York Times* I am going through inspires me to think about our Colonel North and about other terrors today which are described.

What is this like? (No answer.) Is this like anything familiar? (No answer.)

Are you familiar with this? (No answer.)

I will answer that it is the burden. It is intellectual work which is as degrading to do as being in the presence of some very great person.

It is so similar to bowing to regard the genitals.

What is it that I would like right now?—to suck a very clean penis? (Yes.)

I am very embarrassed.

Happy

The child arrived in the nick of time to eat a pancake. She wasn't trying to escape from sadness, and she wasn't dying for a pancake, but she could handle a pancake standing up, without using a plate or a fork.

The wife wasn't eating yet, but she was cooking and preparing to serve. It meant so much to the wife to do that. Her husband would be served. The wife must have given him an ultimatum. He wore pajamas. The wife wore daytime clothes. The child was dressed for the occasion, and wore these sturdy toddler shoes.

Surely it is a fact of experience, that a young enough

child who believes that pancakes are delicious, usually embraces an opportunity to eat one. At the age of two, this child considered her opportunity and made a decision that was plausible to her at the time. However, as an adult who is a happy-go-lucky person for no good reason, she marvels at how jubilant she was, so young, when she missed out on a pancake in a circumstance when nobody preeminent was sneering at her.

The Case of the Cold Murderer

Getting the lid off the stuff, Mrs. Lewis knew, might mean she would save her son's life, so she worked at it. You uncap it in extremis.

The doctor had advised her by telephone to give it to her son. "This will work if you say to him it will work."

Louella Stack always said it was a simple death, this kind, although unexpected. One feature in the matter was Glenn Gould's playing piano to accompany the death. To get him calmed down—not Glenn Gould—Mr. Lewis embraced his gasping son. The mother, Mrs. Lewis, tried so hard to uncap the bottle.

The prescribed medicine, in these cases, tastes lousy.

Not long before he died, the son—who is also a suspect, actually—shrieked as best he could at Mrs. Lewis, "You have hurt me so much! I don't want to be your son! I can't breathe!"

Nobody denied any of this.

But perhaps if I speak to him . . .

Regrettably, the parts you will not hear are the parts that sound the best, as I, your host, shrewdly unravel the tangle of motives and human relations. For instance—I'll mow the fucker down—who is this fucking Stack? Was she really worth the mention?

The Leader

In just a little while I was not yet so weary that I was furiously working on the secret of life, of my life.

The words in my mouth are uncontrollable the way they come out to speak. Fluently I say: He is a Jew, but who am I?

The Jew laughed, and he said coercively, before he stripped himself naked, before he became the master of my body, before he tickled my slit, before he tugged on my slit, before he tugged it, before he tugged on it, before I was so hard on his hard-on—he said it coercively to me: "Don't be so silly."

"You must let go of me," I said.

Wisely, the Jew said, "This is what it always comes to."

I struggled to my feet. I was profusely kind, too, before going any further. Then the Jew got up, too. He is by temperament eager.

We were near a patch of trees where there was a family—I think a family excited by fury. Not one of them—the three little girls, a mother, and a father—looked to me, in any way, calm, or happy, or prepared quite yet to be the leader of the family.

Nor was that all: Underfoot, there were heavy tree roots popping up everywhere, and acorns, some crushed, some with, some without their tiny whatnots still on, all of which—this spectacle—was not useless to me, for I can speak for the Jew, too, such is my destiny, that in full daylight our eyes were open not with horror, not to see a fearful end, but to realize—I realize a certain sort of family should probably gather more often as a group to be a witness to love. It was thrilling when the youngest girl asked me, "Did you ever get caught before?"

"Well, sure," I answered her, "and up yours."

Machinery

He moves around in his gloom and then he does something with something. He is calmer about his longings.

He sits for a bit before he hears whatever it is. Hearing it gives him the sensation of holding on to a great instrument which is at work.

He discovers a small square white cardboard box and he opens it. Inside is a disappointment.

His children hold him responsible for everything he does. His house suits him.

For some idea of the full range of tools at his disposal, one would have to know what human longings are all about, a calm voice says calmly.

Perfect

"You want an insight? I'll give you an insight," said a perfect stranger at the children's ball game. Then he gave me his insight, which proved to be exactly correct.

"People will cheer him when he gets himself up," the man said.

I had thought that the child's ankle was probably shattered—that was *my* insight—that the child would not be able to walk, that he would need to be lifted and carried, that he would never walk again. I thought, Now he is a cripple for the rest of his life.

"He's fine," the man said. "I know he's fine, because, you see, he's hiding his head. He's hiding his face. He's making such a big deal. I know. Sure, it's very painful."

The man had told me that the hardball had hit the child in the ankle. I didn't know where.

I said, "How do you know? It might be shattered. He's not moving."

"Because he missed the ball—" the man said, "because he wants everyone to forget he missed the ball, that's why he's making such a big deal."

If I could have an insight about this man's insight, I could probably save myself. That's my insight. I could save my children, my marriage, the world, if I could let enough people know—that there's a powerful solution in here somewhere—a breakthrough trying to break through.

The stranger was so angry talking to me. I don't think he believed I was believing him, and I didn't.

Will you please rise and Shame us not, O Father.

The Stupefaction

An Opening Chat

I am glad he is this man here so that I can do a fuck with someone, but I am regarded as a better cocksucker. It is one of those lovely times when a crisis does not come as a surprise. That is how I feel. I am glad he is this man here so that I can suck his cock and lick it. This goes on a little longer. I understood everything up to that point. This goes on a little longer. This—this cock is swollen. The throbbing of this cock begins. I felt sorry about what he had to do to me.

After this time, I noticed that I was not the same again as I had once been. I was much more swollen when the doctor arrived.

"We will get you back—we will get you back to where you were when you were feeling strong. Is that what you want?" the doctor asked.

"Yes. I want to feel strong again. I find that giving a blow job takes everything out of me," I said.

"Yes, that's true," the doctor said.

The doctor might believe that with a person of my age he may be blunt.

You would think that it could not last—his wanting to get straight to the point where something ceases to exist.

The Key to Happiness

It would have been very unlike me to be unenchanted very often. Once when the telephone was ringing when I returned home, I was not delighted. This is the way it is often now in my own home. I am so used to it—as if I were in that part of the world where when you are a visitor everything is so enchanting. The radio is not even on very loud. I have turned it off. I am full of contentment. Follow along with me if you are full of contentment also, because then you will be able to understand this. One day I went to a plumbing-supply store. I needed a new faucet for the kitchen sink. The clerks were eating pizza. It was lunchtime. Each customer had to wait at least a half hour before being attended to. I had to wait. The waiting was exquisite, startling, passionate, magical.

The Blessing

I said so in the letter, but virtually anyone could have said so: *You will have everything you want. I don't want to get your hopes up and then disappoint you.*

He just loves me. I have a very bad temper.

I walk forward with the letter in my hand, wearing my black dress, which gently slaps at my legs as I walk forward. For about an hour, I wrote the letter with a dull lead pencil. On the envelope, in ink, dutifully, I wrote the name, the address. The stamp is a large black-and-green one.

Life is curious. I drink half a glass of water. In the corner of the room, rather, in the center of the room, nothing any longer attempts to sing a song, or, on the other hand, is list-less, actually sick to death, and will not recover. But I don't mean this as an incitement to get you to go tell people that everything can turn out happy, wholesome, just wonderful.

One afternoon, when you are particularly tired, you sit down. You will be sitting down, or maybe it will be late in the evening, and you have missed your dinner, and you have missed your lunch, and you have missed out on your break-fast, too, and the weather is hot, so that you feel hot. It is an unhealthy climate, which is humid and stifling, and the air you breathe is unhealthy for you, and then, you obtain your heart's desire.

Many times a person seems fairly satisfied already but is so unsuspecting.

Eero

Tthe twwo pairrs off iddentical chairrs hadd been chosenn byy tthe ownners off tthe hhouse bbecause off tthe strengthh off theirr ccharacter. Thhe chairrs neverr beckonned tthe litttle girrls forr sitting.

Tthese wwere gennuine Eero Saarinen chaiirs— yyou musst takke mmy worrd forr itt—sttanding behindd thhe litttle girrls innside thhe hhouse, fromm wwhere tthe girrls stood tto watcch rrain beeat dowwn onn little apple trees, whichh treees hadd been plantedd byy thee owwners aas ann orrchard, delliberately, beccause tthey looked sso muchh aalike.

Sso thenn, bbecause itt wwas theirr gamme, onne girrl waas saaying, "Ddo whatt II ddo!" tto tthe otther, jjust thhe waay thhe trees seemed tto bee doiing.

Uppon thhe *wwhat* worrd off herr command, thhe otther girrl ssaid thhe *wwhat* alsso. Ttheir *wwhats* coveredd overr themselves, hhers and herrs, andd thhen thhe exxact saame thingg wwas happening tto tther *II doos*, whhich arrived—nno jokke—withh aa majjestic simmultaneity.

Att ourr housse, itt's ggoing onn—anny gamme off tormment—wee still doo itt.

EEEverywhere!

APPPPOLOGY: Itttt wouldddd hhhhave beeeen entirrrrely tooooo tirrrresome forrrr meeee, tttthe onnnne whhhho wrrrrote tttthis, orrrr ffffor anyyyyone whooo rrrreads thissss, tttto havvvve hadddd tooo advvvvance thrrrrough thissss, assss thhhhrough ourrr olllld agggge, allll thhhhe waaaay throughhhh thissss, evennnn thoughhhh thatttt's sssso obbbbviously thhhe waaaay, wiiiith aaaa grimmmm conssssstancy, itttt shouldddd beeee dddddone.

194

The Idealist

Without much enthusiasm, he led me down the corridor and opened the door. He didn't have to say, "I'm the one who did that." I knew. I assume he has been places where he has seen beauty, has had some joy and adventures.

He stumbled. He fell down. I might have struck him, that's why.

People have to do so many things just to live their lives. He probably suffered from the fall, but he acted oddly light-hearted. I am tempted to guess why that is. I owe him an apology, but not if he is never angry with me.

How do other people who don't know each other very

well count their blessings?

While I eat my hamburger, we leave our clothes on because we are very shy. We hardly know each other. We manage to copulate occasionally and to remain ill-qualified.

A Moment of Panic

I am not ecstatic about the flesh on her not-yet-womanly body, and her other arm is very much like her other one, and so on. However, none of her duties are undone, or need doing, or are duties which will soon need doing, which could be vexing. She has no dilemma evincing a religious principle. And, instead of a gang of people fucking her, or poking fun at her fat cunt lips, she has under her feet a luxuriant carpet. In addition, her laundry has been laundered by her, and now, in spite of itself, this laundry is soft and folded, or hanging languorously. Some of her bedclothes are trimmed with a frothy white trim, because people she has never met made a decision that that trim would be nice.

From her side of it, looking anywhere, everything is sunlit, entrancing.

But beyond this recognition, which is mine, not hers, there is this aroma, unsmelt yet by me, blowing around through the cool air here, coming along, mixed with some sudden large gusts of true love, which all you do—you want it?—is on weekends, you inhale it.

O Rock!

I don't wish to be callous or unfeeling. Go out if you like, but don't expect anything, even if we find the packet.

Actually, it is a large padded envelope that the man she follows into the café drops onto the table, then proceeds to undo. He has to break its seal.

She drums her fingers on her chin, watching him.

Her heart beats heavily, for which she is repaid in kind.

A thousand years are accounted for as he turns it upside down, empties out a dime, a penny, a penny, a dime, a dime, a dime. He empties out Time because of her. I am paying attention. Do *you* have to?

I hate it when you're like this.

Luxuries

In a fussy mood, she came home to me. Her arms were gold-looking and cold to the touch when I touched them. The house key she had used to get into my house has a loop of gold cord threaded through it. She slipped my house key into the pocket of my jacket.

Our lives, which are leading us toward the shiny, bright flower of death, are austere, but if she says so, here, she can have money and glamour, she can have it. She can smoke a cigarette, since her husband is not with her, nor her children, nor her boyfriend. She has followed me. The sights we might see through my windows are associated with the mysteries—

animals, automobiles, not much more. I see a cloud-gray auto. I see a rocket-red auto. I see a jet-black animal.

Lois Holway, of Superior Exteriors, called. But I said, "No, I am sorry. We are not interested."

I was too busy being overcome with vain delights to say more. True, too, there was nothing more to say to the Holway woman that would be as true as *I am afraid of you.*

The Guider of the Prick

She wanted Bill to obey her. She wanted that very much. When Bill came down out of the tree, his mother was a little afraid of him, but she said, "Good"—meaning, she was glad that he was back down.

Boy, she thought, is Bill ever a handsome boy. She flung her arms around Bill. Then she tested the skin on her own arm with her fingertips to see if it was still as soft as silk, and it was.

Would Bill's mother ever say to Bill, "You've done enough for me already"?

Bill gets angry now, as a grown man, when some woman

guides his prick for its entry into her cunt hole.

But back to when Bill was the pluckiest little boy in the world, sitting on a tree branch, and his mother had thrown a small rock at Bill, and his mother wept and Bill wept, too. Bill saw apology, sadness, and disbelief in his mother's face. In Bill's face, his mother saw ordinary crying going on.

This is what Bill looks like as of today: He is large and unkempt, with unruly dark hair and dark eyes. His mother is proud of him. He is the keeper of the flame.

Speech

Thank goodness I am deeply sincere, so I stopped laughing. He had dragged me along to this refined filth of a hotel, which aroused my truest false feeling. On the way to the hotel, he was staggering and I was. If my wish is at last coming true, he is going to spring on me something that will make me feel as helpless as a human being.

He'll hear about it now.

A joke he told me had interfered with our breathing. Two women, I don't know, across the street were being dragged into the same experience, too—by a joke, or by something such as a joke.

Maybe he has not figured out yet how much I wish to stiffly represent myself at coital functions as stiffly as I do here as I speak.

For Diane

Very early on, I had a vision of excellence and a sense of responsibility of monstrous proportions.

It is best if no one ever sees me again. (You will thank me.)

I will not go to see someone just because he or she is conveniently located.

And, if you do that thing again, evil people will be ruined completely. Good people will feel great. Springtime will span the year because that's my decision. Anyone who would have preferred some other season may feel a not-so-serious mistake has been made.

When the good people begin their lavish new life, they will be especially indebted to Ira, who will provide everyone with a set of easy instructions to follow so everything turns out all right for them. Oh, they will be indebted to Ira.

I used to see a lot of this one woman. Ira will take care of her, because I've had it up to *here*.

Now, do you understand?

Plural

There is this one where they all put their feet up or slouch, because of the decree.

The worst of this is now over for Irene. She can just relax.

The iridescent ribbon, which might be regarded as pure or perfected, is in her hand. Her knees were drawn up. Her arms were exerting enough of her power.

Maybe she drew her thighs closed. She has soft, thin skin. She is plump because she has been stuffed with pralines, which is the secret of her plumpness. She likes to eat sweets.

She touched her genitals, thinking wistfully that they were flawless.

They are at their succulent best—red and yellow, but still firm—and if the skin is tender, you do not need to peel them. You can have the butcher make a series of fine, shallow cuts on the surface.

The Transformation

An unpleasant light coats all of her submerged body. She bears this coloration also.

After her bath, she feels she is significant. She eats some biscuits. The leftover biscuit morsels she goes ahead and she scrapes off of her plate into the garbage can. The stain on her shoe is hot blue or has been caused by some hot glue. To tell you a lie, even about this last, would be such a waste of everybody's time.

When the woman asks her loving friend, "Are we having that falafel for dinner?" the knife that the woman has been containing vigorously gets playful and she stabs herself with it

mercilessly. She is aroused. She urges herself to think of herself. She says to herself, "You must, you must think of yourself
and no other." She says, "To tell you the truth, you are dead."

Truthfully speaking, the above marvel has been described
irresponsibly, without any perception on my part as to the
why, the wherefores, or even any of the heretofores, or even
why I thought to make the whole thing up. And I am not sorry
for it at all. You deserve everything you get, I am sure, even
the crap you have to read, and of course, this fake woman
hasn't died; she has just transformed herself into me: I am
about five foot three. I am a woman. I am of royal blood and
huge intellect and I enjoy myself immensely, *come hell or
high water!*

It is not in her nature to feel the way I do.

Gods of the Earth at Home

Mr. Moody and I were standing still for the sight, mentioning the sight, leaning slightly, or touching each other.

The soda was fizzing and the redness and the whiteness of the soda were dull compared with the redness and the whiteness of a fine radish.

It was Mr. Moody's boy Jim who had danced in with his bottle of cherry soda, turning the bottle, which was capped, over and over, and shaking the bottle, and the boy was spinning and hopping.

Mrs. Brute deplored the champagne we were drinking. She is my invention. She is going to take care of Jim.

Our exceptional meal was served on the golden plates. The silverware was real silver. Mr. Moody's face flushed when he drew me to him. He touched my beautiful auburn hair and my rich black velvet jacket. I had removed my deep sable. He could not be restrained from embracing me in the full view of everybody.

I just kept saying yes. When he said what he said, I said yes yes yes yes. I say yes yes. I say my excitement is so great, so huge.

I heard Mr. Moody's respiration. I heard him sort of faintly groan as he does sometimes at the very thought of having to eat my twat.

My imagination tells me that for everything which is not rewarding during a day, a heavy price must be paid.

I hope all of this will turn out all right.

What if it did?

It did.

We should all be so pleased that for the time being we must abide with growing up, getting married, having servants, slaves, houses, holidays.

Desperately Trying to Lie Down

Sometimes you were held, fondled, commented upon, weren't you? Yet I was told that nobody else had ever wanted you or had even asked about you, that I was the first one who had asked about you. When I grasped at you, twisted you, I saw some strands of your hair, the rather imprecise sketch of your eye, the overwhelming importance of your eye, and one of your eyebrows desperately trying to lie down sweetly on your brow, and with this view in mind, your face is as composed as my vulva is. I would like to suggest that the smartest, the strongest, the most perfect person in the universe is my property.

I am the dark one, the short one, the thick one, the coarse one, who is so unsatisfied with all of my suggestions.

You said, "Here, let me help you," and there was such a really happy expression on your face that you must have been happy.

I Am a Learned Person

My name is Valery Plum. There is something funny in that. I cannot presume how true to life I am. When I see myself combing my hair, I seem true to life. I am so starkly represented. I try to see through somebody else's eyes, which would be a remarkable view. This is the second day in a row I have tried; that's because I—I am really looking forward to it, because, even though I have no devoted friend—my newborn is pretty, my lips brightly colored, and there's plenty more of that where that came from.

Up the spiral staircase I go to get the baby, who is not big. Only on the inside, the walls of this tower are the color of a butter cookie. *Heh heh heh,* he's wailing. Under these conditions, nothing but children is so much better than custard or genius or fame.

This may be true or false, but here I am.

An entire formula for feeling good is fitting for someone like a bat out of hell like me who does not tolerate flying with any aches or pains.

Miss M. Murray quoted some ingredients in her own book, and a Mr. Trevor Furze confirmed the same in his own. One of their key ingredients is yummy, would make dogs bark. I go up and down the stairs with it in my mouth. It dangles.

I can make it leap up again.

Careful

We could hardly bear it when she arrived home unhurt. The situation had grown intolerable. A week or so after that, we saw her again, still no accidents. She's a young woman. Maybe sometime soon she will be destroyed.

As a matter of fact, just now she is in some peril. She is having a conversation.

Among her lady friends, her masters, her heirs, she shouts, "Charming!" Her voice is high, thin, nasal.

Just before this, we had thought of calling out to her to wait, but she was already waiting.

She had heard the sound of her own voice without any

assistance or advice.

What if we never see her again?

We have nothing for—we have no plans for—we have no ideas for your—we have no wish to make you—we are—we—feel no—Let's just say there are other people, other than her, that we could speak to. We need to match up our feelings to our ideas for them.

Yesterday, we found it charming—all that shooting the semen around that they do.

What Knowledge Is Most Worth Having?

"There you are, Diane," she says, "an omelette."

She sets it down in front of me.

What next?

If light is being shed here, you will know.

My theory is that there is a profound, a gumbo effect that proceeds from one's being anywhere within earshot of the mention of food as a plaything.

Do you ever treat restaurant personnel shabbily?

Beware.

Indeed, personnel in general—Beware, I think—yes, beware of personnel or of any of their friends or their family.

A More Detailed Account of This Is Out of the Question

At the time of crisis, this man has arrived. Anything more I describe might give the wrong impression about his perfect timing, but that's too bad—how he has just appeared on the floor, lying down; another time at the back door, entering; once when I was down on my knees. Another time, we stood on the stairs. Once when I was leaning against the drawer in which I keep the flatware, he was with me.

I wanted to moan with my delight. But it would have confused him, because he says, "Are we there yet?"—the only words he will say in reply to anything ever.

I have never seen such a dignified man as he is. He has a

pained expression on his face. His breathing is labored breathing. When he reaches my cartographer's side, the fellow is awake, sitting up.

It is so easy to get a boyfriend. By the light of the sun, I watch them. I get used to watching what I should have. Repetition of this kind is not lulling.

The Fuck

The pungency, the mystery, the awesomeness of his idea was terrific. Mother of God—he actually had a cloth and a spray bottle of something, because he was dusting his truck. His truck was blocking up our street that we live on.

As I ran away from him, I shouted, "I am not trying to run away from you!" Brutally, I kicked what I decided was my own stone, and I found a limp walking stick—a dead tree branch, smooth, just the right height—after it was boring for me to be brutal.

Ferocious, hateful dogs, working as a team, barked at me.

What are the Williamses putting that up for? I wondered, when I turned my corner. Now, he was over there, in their yard, not looking at what he was doing with their swing set, speaking only to me, when I came along.

There was no mention of being ill or an illness mentioned which was of an extreme or of a debilitating nature. Pleasure was the centerpoint, sexual pleasure, fun, surprise, gamy delight—seldom—well, all right, *once!*—disgust. He did not express desire other than sexual, which he was confident he would gratify soon. He had no concern that any woman, man, girl, or boy would not be a good-enough provider for him, or could somehow disappoint him, or turn up incompetent. Beauty, intelligence, education, gentility, cleanliness, worldly success, a moral attitude—none of these he ever referred back to. No concern over betrayal, no money problem was expressed, and yet, even so, I behaved curtly. I behaved as if he had digressed.

The Goal

"I want to use yours."

"Use any bathroom you want to," she said.

He said, "Oh, you are my friend!"

He put his hand between her legs. He said, "Come. Sit up here. Back—*back*—"

He mouthed her; he tongued her; he nosed her between her legs. He murmured, "Let go."

"Oh, that was a treat!" she said. She stood. She stood on tiptoe and she embraced him.

"I have to go to the bathroom," he said.

"Use the children's," she said.

He twisted to gaze at her while she was not straining to be anything more than what she is. He was free and happy, too. In her bathroom, she was reaching to turn the little spinner, to twirl the screw propeller which releases some of the water through the bunghole into the remarkable.

My Reaction to Life

Our half-broken horses were rearing and whinnying, their blackened figures brutish and inhuman. Some of their rumps were being slapped.

I tore off my gloves. My hands were warm. Although, the largest single hot body among us, I bet, was Harry Winch's brown horse, Drifter. It is hard to describe these animals which are so stiff-necked.

I stroked my horse, told it to stand still. I can be indifferent and patient. I am one of those who keeps expecting the dark heart of human desire to be revealed to me.

Others were looking down into the gorge, with their

mouths agape.

Chet Henry said, "Now what?" and there is no going back and changing what he said, because that is what he said. He is a man who may have temporarily gotten off of his horse so that he could be loved, or so that he could be hated, or so that he could hate me.

Now what? I am going to answer him the only way I know how. I said, "We're going back to the ranch." The ranch has real log buildings, cowboys, excellent meals.

Nobody has to tell me how we made it back through the thicket to the Ridn-Hy. The traveler in me is full of hope. She is a splendidly bland and a smug woman.

The Dirty Necklace

She used the bath mat to dry the wet necklace, and dirt
from the necklace showed up on the bath mat. She could wash
the necklace again. She put some bar soap on the necklace,
not too much, and then she rinsed the necklace. She repeated
this. The necklace could be washed again. The necklace could
be scrubbed with a scrub brush. The necklace should soak
overnight in a basin. She dried the necklace by rubbing
it against the bath mat, so that more dirt showed up on the
bath mat. She put the necklace on. She fingered the necklace
and saw that its parts were cut glass, amber, or plastic.
The necklace was meant to be hers. We do not know who

else, if anyone, has ever worn the necklace. There are other necklaces which she owns—not exactly the same—but these necklaces are a series of misunderstandings—as is every-thing—at your throat.

The Masturbator

We are all so much the same—our size, our shapes, and we are perforated. I put my finger on a crack in my skin. I have been searching for one gesture of my own such as this which I can remember—return to, and return to, which could direct and give sense to my life. I had ignored other motions of my heavy body—the lowering and raising up of my hind end, which I often do. My legs are tired, and I feel weak-kneed, and it looks to me that there is a place to sit down to rest near a tree. This tree's trunk is a subtle tawny color. The ground is dark, has speckles. I press on my hand. I am still not uncertain what to think when I gently rub my hand, which seems to me dirtfree and oldfangled. There are much more up-to-date revealers of the truth.

Okeydoke

The man lied is the best ingredient in my veal steak deluxe. I am going to vacation in the man lied. I never will the man lied for the third time.

I the man lied that that's wonderful and exciting and I look forward to it. He is telling me how many the man lied he has to have in a day.

I expected to the man lied blood.

The man lied, "I have never seen the man lied like that one."

On the man lied, when some chicken and a potato were roasting in my oven, I would not leave the man lied. I liked to tell the man lied how many orgasms I had in a day.

The man lied was sure I was hearing a waterfall. But what I heard was the grinding of the man lied.

The Fuss

First of all, I do not want to keep the thing a secret, because they were not doing any harm, I assure you. They ate. They drank heartily. They threw stones which sank into the sea. They jumped into the sea. We followed them. The sea was bright and whirring. I was not used to being cold in the water. I am not used to keeping a secret, either, which I think is the best plan. It was a journey. There was a beautiful sky. We were too cold creeping under it. A little farther on, they marched. I cannot form an idea from this.

Thank You

A margay has heavy black eyebrows, heavy, black, wavy hair. An ocelot is very much the same. No margay has been seen around here, but we were determined to find one if it is in the books. We crouched in a field studded with hares and cows and dogs. We were in extreme agony because we were bewildered and we had been wandering. (I was in a very bad mood.) Several of us have long, gray, matted hair and are extremely ugly. I wear a black skullcap. An odd-looking stranger (but what stranger isn't?) hobbled up to us and told us what to do. She squatted. Her knees bumped into her shoulders. She told me to think about something else for a change.

The Primary Intuition

We have conspicuous yet, I think, respectable hair on our heads. Even so, my son and I could scare people. We have. We walk along. I see scarlet-fruited, big-leaf winter creeper, inkberries. At last, we arrive at the village. I knew what we would do, where I would accompany him.

Pierre and Esther, our enemies, entered a shop. I had seen Esther, with her trailing spray, wearing her *sautoir*, open the door. The light spreading rapidly from the shop windows was not warm and inviting.

We had the advantage of staying close to the building.

By the time we left town, I had an invisible ring on my

finger, as well as a strong brown cut, which has the appearance of an aeriel rootlet. I had watched my son drink from a swaying glass of juice, which is perfumed, forms in clusters, turns yellow, before it comes into sight.

The Builder

I drank dark water, later on, afterward. I urinated, emitted gas. I was pleased, tired, had cramps. I could not stop the monster from causing its destruction. It had left no real damage after the cleanup. Out of devotion? Because of fear? Or pride? I often have an outburst of my free will. I know what I will do if I have sexual intercourse, how I am going to hump and plan. I suspect many others need to plan your sexual intercourse.

The Answer to the Question

A coil of green, a part of me, or any additional garnishing, when assembled, can produce sufficient allure anyplace.

The old idea that enticements should be ever more sophisticated is what prevents most seers—plumbers and electricians alike—from being optimistic.

Keep on hand containers which you have filled compactly. Wrap these securely. A stream or a flow is a thing of the past.

The Suitor

We are becoming persons who should, of course, be loved and honored. We become people who can do the impossible.

Was anyone surprised to see us take on a different shape and character? In the name of everything which is sacred, I can predict your fate to ensure that you will never worry.

I am your friend, if you do what I tell you to do. Don't worry.

Let's pretend I have made mistakes. Let's pretend that these sorts of mistakes are the ones I never should have made. I have no respect for you, for instance. I think I can just pick up anything of yours and look at it. I hear myself shout, "That's the trouble!"

The Stupefaction

One Place
Same Place
Everything
For
You

Is it necessary to state
a guarantee of my goodwill?

If they come in, they go
right back out again.

—SEVERAL OF MY NEIGHBORS

❊ 1 ❊

Oh, I Hope You Like Everything I Say!

Somewhat embarrassed, he would not admit that he wanted to do something with her right away which might surprise her or possibly cause her some pain.

"I came directly here!" he said. His sad expression had vanished. He said, "Let's go!"

They did not take her little dog with them. It is dangerous to show her dog too much affection, she believes. This could cause harm.

She had another one of her own ideas when she saw a pool of some forgotten water, when she saw some of the forsaken hills. She said, "This is the nicest part of the trip!"

More of her own ideas occurred to her when they were up in the hills.

If she is not much different than I am, she was hoping I would like everything she would say.

He frowned. He said, "We must hurry." He said, "Go on ahead."

By this time, it was twilight. They could barely see the ground or the form of a person doing something patiently and carefully. This apparition is what she has so often feared. She said, "I think that that looks real."

They were struggling. He said, "I'm not sure I like this whole thing. Can't you hurry?"

✳ 2 ✳

This Heavenly Life Is Not Forbidden

"I'll try," she said.

She felt the need to urinate.

They crossed the bridge on foot, and they entered the woods.

This heavenly life is not forbidden.

"We don't know a thing about these woods," she said. "It is heavenly." She sighed, wondering about his bobbing cock.

Something else crawled away and hid under a log. Something else brushed his side. She had had to shoo them off.

He begged her to let him keep on talking.

He likes it when she is acting as if she is nice and

friendly, when he is imagining he wants to be with nobody else.

Amazingly, they did not lose their way in the woods. Yet neither of them had the ornament that wards off evil and that could bring either of them good luck.

When she squatted down to urinate behind a tree, she listened to her noise. A trickle of her urine wet one of her shoes. She had a tissue with her so that she could wipe off her shoe that had been wetted.

Once in the course of her entire lifetime, she almost saw where that urine of hers pours out from.

But no, sorry, she never did actually exactly see.

She was summoning more pleasure when she heard the squirrels.

These squirrels are so fidgety. A few of these squirrels were becoming violently ill and would have very little privacy when this was the case.

Meanwhile, far away, in her garden, her dog was chewing on a rosy green pear that he held between his paws, and not at all tenderly. The dog was gnawing, biting, on the pear as if it were his own flesh and blood!

In the evening, she put her hand down inside her blouse and there between her breasts there was a little something which she would set free.

❋ 3 ❋

It Was a Joyful Time

She pulled out the honest soul but did not examine it before she tossed it away.

It was a joyful time.

Soon she had a fire going in the fireplace.

They have located this ideal cottage. This cottage has been created to augment, to ease an intimate relation, to provide long-lasting help, to reduce the possibility of sin. She will never be one of those people who is slain.

He's probably happy. He is probably happy.

He has something in his hand.

She is trying to give herself something more to be grateful

for than only just some spasms up inside of her cunt. Oh, I love this! she must be saying.

She is hoping to understand anything.

She'd like to tell him, Stay there where I put you.

He was opening the drawers—drawer after drawer.

The cottage had been prepared for them, or so it seemed to them—firewood in a basket, a packet of matches, common white spring blossoms in a vase, soap, towels, food, clean bedding—everything!—even a freshly laundered blue terry-cloth robe was there! Before long, the cottage has lost its chill.

She followed him into the kitchen and watched him open a cupboard door.

A surprise clattered.

❄ 4 ❄

Cautiously, She Looked Around

She did not remain calm. "I think you've done enough searching!" she exclaimed.

He believed that everything was so cosy. Soon enough, there was the fragrance of cream.

In the kitchen, she had prepared a full-fledged cocoa bread pudding.

An insect drifted up before her eyes, then flew away. She briefly inspected the ether for the insect. Then she looked for a miracle of beauty high up in the air in the out-of-doors.

He lit beeswax candles—dripless, clean-burning—which produced soft light.

"That's ours!" he said when she found a jar of red jam. She saw him steadily stride. She thought, I know I can trust him.

Orange sparks sprang up the way they usually do when he interfered with the fire.

On the hearth was a pair of lady's dancing slippers, of delicate dark velvet, covered by gold embroidery and braid and daisy patterns made of ivory-colored small pearls, as well as a pair of man-sized, wide-topped, funnel-shaped half boots of embroidered leather.

Offering him his pudding, she said, "This is so cosy!"

These are people who are often alone together. Perhaps they could be cruel, useless people, incapable of understanding very much about anything.

Cautiously, she looked around.

This may be a trap.

✷ 5 ✷

Don't Start Imagining Things

"Don't start imagining things," he said while he was slumped, eating his dessert, in the chair, his trousers lowered to his ankles. "This is so cosy," he said. He believed that he had thought of the idea of cosiness all by himself.

"It is eerie, though," she said.

Contents of the drawers were scattered on the floor.

He chuckled.

She did not ask for an explanation, such as, What amuses you? She never ever wants to be the kind of woman who causes him to be cross, who speaks harshly to him.

Just as she was attempting to handle another one of her

concerns, the telephone rang. She had forgotten about sexual pleasure. The ringing reminded her.

When the telephone was ringing, he said, "Uh-oh!"

She grabbed his arm and then she guided him through the cottage. He was using his knees to hold up his flapping trousers. She was behind him, her hands on either side of his waist. "In here," she said powerfully, flinging the door open, pushing him forward.

❆ 6 ❆

She Put the Lid of the Toilet in Place

"Don't do that," he said.

After all, he had invited her to come with him because he had thought that he might have some fun.

If the telephone rings and rings, or if there is knocking at the door, this is alarming. The telephone is an obdurate potentiality.

When he was stepping into the bathtub, which was brimming with the same sort of water she is accustomed to, she worried.

What should I do? I should do something, she fretted.

He made no comment. She did not see his face. She was

not at all certain that she was in fact supposed to lightly touch him in this circumstance, or to grip him otherwise.

She put the lid of the toilet in place, then she watched him from her perch on the toilet lid.

In this same room, she had earlier moaned, "What am I going to do?"

She is just here to make herself happy.

"I want to touch you," she said.

"Fine," he said. "Do it wherever you want."

She put her finger on the tip of his penis and she pushed it down. She bent his penis.

"Can I kiss you?" she asked.

"Fine," he answered.

So she did.

She kissed his brow; then she petted the top of his head.

"Do you want me to stop?" she asked.

"No," he said.

He said no.

❈ 7 ❈

She Was Alert to Her Terror

She kissed his waxy pate many times.

"Oh," he said, sighing, "where did you learn to do that?"

She was sure she should not answer this question. This is the oldest, the most difficult, question.

Meanwhile, the night advanced. This had been confirmed when she was sitting on the rim of the bathtub, since she could then see out the window.

She was alert to her terror but was only faintly informed of her total helplessness.

His knees were up near his chin. He looked so handsome to her naked.

She flinched when he spoke. She did not know what to say, so she is quiet. She had nothing to offer that might reveal the secret meaning of things—the truest things.

It is easy to forget that during the next two days she solved the only problem that remained for her to solve, at which time she did say, "I thought of that all by myself!"

If anyone had entered the room, such a person might have been curious. Probably at times he had wondered, What is the matter with us?

Her interest in teasing him startled her.

"Oh, yes, I want to," she said.

❋ 8 ❋

She Appreciated It So Much Whenever He Tried to Please Her

Earnestly, he kept on having these sexual sensations.

He was feeling better, although he was still afraid of being scolded.

When he got up out of the tub of water, he predicted some horse sense, some magic, and some wishful thinking.

She asked, "Are you going to get into that bed with me?"

He answered yes, that he was.

Since she knows in general what to do, she did not feel ill-tempered, even though her first efforts to please him usually did not work.

She appreciated it so much whenever he tried to please

her.

When he gleefully played with her, this might not have been a dream.

He did not remember that he had not done anything of this kind in a very long time.

He is so weary of trying to remember anything, because prior to this escape from his life, his life had been one of the most wearying lives ever lived. Presumably, his life had occasioned a type of slave labor.

He said, "I bet nobody has ever done this!"

"I don't know," she said. "Just stick it in and I will think about it."

❋ 9 ❋

She Was Soiled—but Wetted?

The accounts of how she lost her dignity vary. She does not know that she is vehemently inclined to be made happy at any cost.

Force it on me, she is craving, and please forgive me for anything I could ever do that is wrong or that I have already done that is wrong, and forgive me for what I am doing right now!

She is slack-faced, flushed, after that. She has a sense of a heartening achievement.

"That's it, my darling," he said. "If I were your mother, I could not be prouder of you."

To her surprise, when she was not asleep, he reached out and insinuated his arm around her!

Late that night, water is running. He must have been getting into the bathtub again. Oh, the nice bathroom.

Remember, nothing really terrible is ever supposed to happen to her.

She was soiled—but wetted?

She was the only person she had ever heard of she could envy.

About half an hour later, he approached her. His purpose was to kiss her lovingly. He said her name sweetly, which caused her to feel very fortunate.

Perhaps this should have been brooded over—what her name is.

Her eyes, ears, nostrils, mouth, anus, legs, and other parts of her are wrongly formed.

Her skin is extraworn, extrafaded, extraunfirm. Her character, her intellect, her health are relevant but not known now.

He is the same size she is, or he is much smaller than she is. His skin is so different from hers.

He is gentle. He is nervy, but this is not all that he is.

✤ 10 ✤

Outside, Everything Is Spectacular

He is terrific.

His robe is something I have worn. It is a deep dark blue robe, rude, but not handmade. If someone were to take his robe seriously, his robe might appear to be ongoing, as if this terry-cloth robe could stand up to the test of time, or to the open air.

Outside, everything is spectacular.

Inside, the man and the woman chat a little, laugh quite a bit. They may question each other. Also, they answer each other. They can be sexually pleased. They bathe. The man cleans the kitchen floor more carefully than he has ever cleaned himself.

At this point, far, far away, the woman's everlasting dog cannot remember how he used to pity himself.

Her dog will not be lonely. There cannot be another plan other than this plan for her dog's future.

The dog considers himself superior to other dogs.

Other creatures could be accounted for as well, with vulgar praise, or there will be public disappointments.

The question is, What more should this man and this woman do there in that house? All of the usual methods of sexual intercourse can be delightful, especially if done with care.

Behold! The man is going to give the woman something!

It is a ruby ring, which fits her, with a single ruby as shiny as mine is, which he discovered in a cake pan—and he gave it to her.

Imagine! The woman can hear the splashing and the rippling of the light inside the gem!

She groans. She shrieks.

This ruby has been dripping with blood once upon a time!

The woman takes a puff of the man's hair in her hand when she says to him, "Oh, thank you!"

Oh, why did I ever let her into the cottage? Was it because she is prayerful?

❉ 11 ❉

She Is Nice, but She Has Aged

She is nice, but she has aged. Now she is pulling her blouse about her. But she is not sad.

I think there is a storm outside—wind and rain. Dirt is blowing into the cottage from under the windowsills. The amount of dirt, the power of the wind, is a bit of a shock to me.

A lot of age-old dust is turning itself into black water around here.

The man's palm is on a windowpane. So is his nose, until he notices that it is.

My worrying about this will not be helpful.

❅ 12 ❅

He Said, "Look Over Here!"

To him, the most enthralling prospect is the most satisfying. He said, "Look over here!" He motioned for her to come closer. "Come over here!" he said.

To her, of course.

The moment has now arrived.

Now, for an excellent moment, they are both gazing at the murk. He is a brave man.

"What is it? What is it? What is it?" she begged of him. "Will you answer a question?"

Once he exclaimed, "What is this?"

They both saw what they should see.

When did this exertion of their vision ever take place?

It took place as my spirit soared, when I observed that they did not want to look at each other.

There was the scent of a charred lamb chop, but there was no indecency in this fact, either.

I saw a sign of some life—and luxuriant shadows—when the door blew open. It was a body with a slender neck, a darting head.

❧ 13 ❧

I Saw It Entering

I saw it was dressed.

The man raised his voice, nearly lost his reason crying out to it, but no answering voice came back to him.

It was necessary now for me to be reassuring. Every moment still counted. I was curious, too, and I was intrigued by the suddenness of its entry. But I was certain we were all still safe here.

A sound not unlike castanets started up. Then, as things will, it stopped.

Within less than an hour, I promise you, this visitor was capable of feelings and was yearning to steal back to its own people.

The man screwed up his courage. He went up to it boldly. This is what I want to do.

The newcomer was so close, I could have touched it. The face of it was somewhat adorable.

Sometimes I heard gasping, or a heavy footfall, which could not have lasted for more than for a few instants.

In my opinion, this creature had stumbled into a trap.

❧ 14 ❧

You Should Have Seen What I Saw

Its profile is remarkably like my mother's.

You should have seen what I saw, for this thing was not much larger than you could manage to see.

The man went to clutching at it. He was trying to hold on to whatever he could, to take it into his hands.

At first, all that he could see was a vague shimmering, which he could have been undone by. Yet, the older, the stronger, we are, I think, the greater our sense of wonder.

The woman saw it appear when the dearie's hands were held above the head—then again when it was folding its palms together, trying to keep its chin up.

❇ 15 ❇

It Was a Golden Structure

I knew that I would have to make proper use of this radiance. It was a golden structure—brighter than any of my daydreams.

With my step-by-step intervention, especially that all concerned should keep on breathing in their fashion, I tell you that the woman thought to place in front of it a small dish of condiment.

"I think I'll sample a bit of this," it said.

Oh—but oh, oh, oh.

Choking, having done so, it declared, "I have been killed."

❦ 16 ❦

He Said, "Look! Here's Something! This May Be Valuable!"

"A little of that goes a long way," the man said. He gave it something to drink.

"Have a glass of this," he said.

And eventually this substance proved to be soothing.

Mentioning that it would return again soon, this dream come true was able to disappear gracefully back into its origin, but not before the three of them had achieved a certain sense of society with one another.

And while it had seemed that the darling had actually put the toxin into its mouth, in fact, this had not been the case.

By the time I had forgotten about the interruption, the old house seemed snug again to me.

I could see clearly the faces of the man and the woman—because I needed to.

He had found a few more treasures.

Some of the bracelets are huge.

He was whispering—but he was not whispering to me!—"How's my darling?"

He was unbuttoning, unzipping, pushing everything down.

When he throws his arms around the woman, he does not know when to let go of her, so that he has to guess when he should.

He should never know absolutely.

So far, he has made some correct judgments, which it will never be possible for him to forget.

He has not washed up any of their dishes or attacked any of the more puzzling tasks.

Nearly everything he ever does gives me a lewd thrill.

He was taking off the woman's old shoes, even though she was telling him, "I'll take it off." They are the kind with laminated leather inserts and fabric laces.

You know.

❧ 17 ❧

"Do You Want to Help?" She Asked

She is behaving as if she is a pleasant woman. She says, "There is a way you can help me."

He is frightened when she tells him how to do this.

He said, "Oh, no, not this time!"

Who would have thought he would be braver than he usually is?

He goes back along a corridor into the bathroom, and she follows him. They are just like ordinary people—and it's not funny!

They must show each other their real shapes, their true skin. They have to.

I am impressed by what lies in store for them, which includes this current adventure of theirs, as well as another expedition.

She washes herself. She combs her hair. She may be deeply in love, as well. I think she is so beautiful.

Oh my God! He is emptying his bowel into the toilet right before our very eyes! But in spite of everything, it is really worth it to him! He has a strong, well-controlled method of defecating.

This event has gotten her strangely worked up.

Let me say that the scent of this man is fantastic, distinctive! It is nutty and sweet.

The linens—the towels in the bathroom—are not stained! There is a blot of something awful in the sink.

He asks, "You look sad. Are you sad?"

❦ 18 ❦

He Said, "Oh, No, Not This Time!"

She is not sad.

She is nice.

At some point soon, she will be down on her back, with her knees up against her tits.

The man tries to remember what to do next.

"Don't forget whose idea this was! It was my idea!" he says.

Nothing too fancy. That's the beauty of it!

"Are you afraid of something?" he asks.

She is afraid to think about what she is afraid of. She feels an urge which even I should not be at liberty to disclose.

All through the wild night, they expect the wind to be blowing.

The murmur of peaceful waters starts up somewhere else. Thick foliage is being crushed underfoot.

She fingers the hair on her head, which to her is stiff and dry—and she is right, it is, it is.

He doesn't insist, although he did feel an impulse rise up in his throat.

"I will stop it right there," he told himself, and he obeyed himself.

The sparse, messed-up hair on her head, her legs, that most unsightly site between her legs would soon be prodded and disturbed.

Where's peace?

The greatest feeling of satisfaction, the way to deepen the experience for her, would be not to let her legs move very far apart, or, in fact, to go ahead and let her legs do that.

She will become aware of how this maneuvering, or absence of maneuvering, can procure a beneficial result.

There are some people who cannot get.

His twitching—his very best flesh—is in her fist.

✱ 19 ✱

He Did Not Know If He Should Be Thinking

He did not know if he should be thinking.

I think they are going to have their dinner—keep the meal simple. She is serving a heavy, sweet pudding. She pours the milk. He is saying, "Just look at this."

Out beyond, in a not so thickly wooded place, a flying thing is buzzing around an ultrasexy flower. Here, too, is the sloping wall of a cavernous pit, with a post at its center— many feet long—which has been sharpened at the exposed pole for one of us.

Suddenly, I had a comforting thought: I am not usually as willful as I used to be.

A matchstick bursts into flame while the woman holds the matchstick. This is the way of things.

The man is glancing at their food. He checks to remember a skillet peach dumpling, a folded rug, or folded food.

She did not sit with him when he drank something.

He is pointing at her.

✹ 20 ✹

His Spirits Were High

He astonished her. There was flirtation. Neither of them is bored with either of them.

She wanted to keep on seeing his helike face.

So do I.

She wanted to keep on being very kind to him. She didn't think she could do this.

Out through the window, anytime of the day or night, there are any number of divinely inspired events which I have not been invited to.

She renews her strength with a silly notion, after pulling off her sock. She holds on to the sock for dear life.

"Please go back to what you were doing," he says.

Her other foot is still up inside of her sock.

Or down inside of it.

"What is this?" he says, indicating.

❄ 21 ❄

At First, She Saw Nothing Unusual

"Is it a door to a secret room?" he asks her. "What do you mean?" she says.

She shuts the door to the broom closet.

This happened the day before I decided to leave them alone, before I decided to leave off pestering them.

She puts on those brand-new slippers that are not characterized by a rear opening and have an almost complete lack of heel.

She says, "You are my favorite person. How do you like that?"

She is warning him with such confidence, wondering

what her words could mean.

At first, she saw nothing unusual.

A few shoots of dark hair on her belly can be seen on her belly.

The door to the kitchen stands open, where fragile porcelain, of various cherished colors, is streaked with a fricassee.

A small figure from another world needs my permission for a taste of something. I signal—to show—that this will be okay.

"Don't forget whose idea this was!" the man is saying to the woman. "Mine, you thief!"

"We can speculate," she answers.

She is . . . well, carefree.

She is nearly naked, being pulled by her arm.

That light hissing I hear when the arm of her blouse is sliding off of her is so exquisite this time that I cannot help wondering why I never paid attention to it before.

This is not anything like music, melancholy or otherwise.

This precious release cannot lull us to sleep, although I can hardly stand up or even keep sitting here any longer.

The man's trousers fell down around his ankles again, covering his footwear and accessories.

Now everything they will do must be complicated and time-consuming because he is fucking her.

She had just become very responsible. Now she wants to feel weaker, weaker, weaker, weaker.

Perhaps the secret concerning sexual intercourse, which she does not know, has made her secretive.

❊ 22 ❊

Imagine!

"Were you here?" the man was asking of somebody.

What if he was asking me?

"I just have to know!" he was saying. "Were you here this time?"

I do not know what more to say—so I could have stopped myself from speaking.

Why don't they just live and live here? Imagine! He doesn't even have to answer the telephone!

Within a few weeks, he had told her, "Sit down."

I think it was for sex.

She pretended to sit.

He was afraid. He drank some cold beef tea. Everything about the tea was unbeatable. It was the best tea.

Why could she not leave well enough alone?

I wanted to believe that she has an elegant mind. But she just doesn't.

She watched him watch her. This is what is keeping her aroused—her pigeon-blood, cushion-shaped gemstone.

I am so proud of that ruby.

The man tries to grasp the meaning of what he should do next.

The telephone is ringing.

Even though I do adore almost any racket, I always think that this kind is tiresome.

I was wishing for my own home a thousand times.

Some of the woman's hair hung down over her face. One of his hands was on top of her head. Both of her hands were on one of her knees. They had torn the blankets and the pillows from the bed.

Then themselves.

✻ 23 ✻

She Will Take a Big Breath

I found out what she was supposed to do next: behave as if she is enjoying the experience.

She says, "Thank you."

I cannot imagine saying some of the things that she brings herself to say.

"But—I don't believe it," he said. He said, "I don't believe it."

Neither one of these people is the one who gives me a reason to live on when there is no other reason. It is somebody else!

Any day this woman will be down on her back, with her

knees up. She will take a big breath. She will be encouraged when he plugs up her awry anus with his straight penis.

❊ 24 ❊

Did He Stand Up Just to Look Around?

Yes, I could see that there had been that hunger in her to feel herself split in half.

I do not want her to know what he is ashamed of.

On top of the toilet tank, there is a filbert, and a cherry stone lying in an openly ostentatious box inlaid with jewels. Part of a walnut is clinging to its smashed shell in the waste bin.

She has herself pressed against the door. "What are you doing? What do you think you're doing?" she is asking him.

He is sitting on the toilet with his elbows on his knees. Then he leaps up.

It is just terrible to see him this way.

But she is still curious to learn more about gentleness, about courtesy—and I do have a fondness for this place because of the stuff strewn all over it.

❋ 25 ❋

It Is Just Such an Unpopular Thing to Do

Even in this bathroom there is a skinning knife!

In every nook and cranny of this cottage there is something that appeals to me.

Will she miss it here as much as I do when I go away?

Did the man stand up just to take a look about and let his thing be seen?

She says, "Wash it."

They really haven't had much privacy. But they have so much time on their hands!

And I do, too!

"You take your time," a kind gent said once so sincerely

as he labored to provoke me with his caresses, for heaven's sake.

A big brute stood by us to keep up our morale.

I did not think I knew either one of them. But nearly everyone I know resembles someone I have known or someone that I know.

The men, the woman, the children are just unfamiliar enough to me so that I do not mind telling any one of them to take as long as it is necessary.

It is just such an unpopular thing to do, though, to take forever to come.

26

I Could Do That

When you are inside of me, this is not unlike my reaching down into a barrel or a big pail for something which I want which is out of my reach, but the barrel needs to be knocked over onto its side.

I could do that.

I graze the back of her hand with the tail end of his penis. Somebody might think that this is true before it is true. I should have always known that I could satisfy her.

When I was confused, he poked a finger up into her vagina.

This time, at least, I am not waiting for matters to be made clear.

27

I Bend Down

When I sat down on top of him, having put his impressively distinct penis up inside of her, everything was what I hoped it should be.

I told him that nobody could fill her shoes.

I had to say things to her that I have never said before.

Every night I would have sat up late, by the fire, so horribly worried about this fact. But that was in the old days.

In the afternoons, if the weather is acceptable for this work, we will think even more about you.

Did I already tell you about the bugleweed that climbed up over the log?

Now the weed heads for the mossy bank, for shade which is too shady for any grass. It is twisting itself up beside a brownish material, climbing up over the log, all because I intend to bend down.

I bend down. I am hearing the rain. I am wishing you well because there is more to come.

❋ 28 ❋

You Will See Me

You will see me not stop being a visitor who could cause a difficulty to such an extent that we would have to handle the ensuing catastrophe, which is ticklish—get some other people to try to get me to pay attention to us.

For example, my mother is a woman who believes my father is more powerful than I am.

My usual rule about building a life or a vase is that it must be slightly tapered.

Most objects require form, don't they?

Small rarities, which are strongly made, well braced, pasty, jellylike, soupy enough, or which are the correct distance apart, will increase in size.

One day, when I walked along the street, I saw my brother carrying a chair.

One of the ears of the chair and the top rail of it, the chair, were scratched. A stile was scratched. The apron of the chair was scratched. One of the finials of the chair had broken loose, was wavering. A joining looked well joined.

My brother had the chair hoisted over his head.

I am not saying there was anything more to this since there was no weather, no water, no barren plain, no rill, no cleft, nor any hillock for as far as my eye could see, and the central peak is so far off.

My brother is somebody I am shy with, who is my idea of a friend, although I hate the nature of everything he is.

If I say that he is really my brother, then I could say nothing is wrong with me except for the aches and pains.

He put down the chair on the sidewalk.

"That's a very nice necktie," I said. "Do you always wear that necktie? You always have on a nice necktie. Is it the same necktie?"

"No, this is a different one," he said.

"You look wonderful," I said. "I can't remember you looking as good as you look."

"Fuck you," he said.

His little girl tugged on the back of his shirt. She was chattering. She—she wants to tell me everything she can think of which is more interesting than anything that you or I could ever think of.

There is a cure for everything.

❋ 29 ❋

I Should Be Carried Off

Considering my increasing interest in, and my knowledge of, the most distant future, I should be carried off for a rendezvous to a place that has an undulating surface, which is inconceivably swampy along the coast—to a life I might not imagine, where there can be some volcanic activity, some full understanding of human health and disease.

The largest city there, which is located in a cultural and medical center, has a great deal of quarried pink quartzite, which I know I like. There is a lake there, too, far above water level, in a sunken volcanic crater. Camellias bloom at the lakeside among live oaks, and azaleas. This is where the temperatures and the humidity have combined to produce the newest conditions.

I still intend to meet up often with you. You listen through thick and through thin. You urge me on. I thank you. I thank you. I thank you. It is high time to give you a complicated sentence.

If you think I will never see you, you are wrong.

✺ 30 ✺

But It Isn't Urgent

I will see you!

At this time, I am staying with friends. It is difficult to get into the bathroom. My sister never says, Don't run the washing machine at all hours.

My sister, my husband, they should offer me a drink.

"Let's have a drink," my sister says.

If it had been urgent, I would have told you that it was urgent. But it isn't urgent.

My sister asked my husband if he would go to the market to get us something to consume.

He said, "Eat this."

She did not say, Could you go now?

He never went off.

No major damage to life or to property otherwise occurred.

But I learned a lesson I will never forget.

31

As It Turns Out

I will encourage myself to lead a more up-to-date way of life, in a rarer atmosphere, where something in the world is really wanted or needed.

People either like me or they don't. Nobody is ever completely persuaded or enthusiastic, though.

Many of those who have thought that they enjoyed my company have not, in fact, been charmed, as it turns out.

I think that they pretend to be in heaven, which is rather romantic.

Heaven all around us, I am fond of saying.

My husband gave me something which demands something.

He said, "See?"

    I put it on.

    He said he had paid for it.

    I wear it, paying for it, too.

✻ 32 ✻

And Now

This is the happiest day of my life, even when I remember this day.

I start for home.

"And now," I say to myself, "never for as long as I live will I ever forget this happiness!"

What do you suppose? I feel I am an important person continuing on my way to do something very important for evermore.

It seems too strange a coincidence to be true that I should get so distracted by you on this day, as if I had carefully planned it that you would show up.

I confess I have always wished that you would be my friend, even though you are a fucking dirty Jew sort of person.

We are as friendly as I have ever been with anyone.

I appreciate how much I want you because I wish that I can appreciate it.

I talk to you very solemnly. You seem to listen, calmly, as I offer you my home, my protection, my love for the rest of my life.

I would like to let go of your arm.

✸ 33 ✸

Just As a Joke

I put my lemonade on a table.

I try to run past you, just as a joke, but you catch me up in your arms.

After a while, you say hoarsely, "I wish I lived here."

"But you do!" I tell you. "We have a lot to be thankful for."

I haven't been complaining. After all, something seems to have happened.

Did you think you would not be invited back?

❦ 34 ❦

I Am in Love

You should know, if you want to come with, that what I am going to do now is go to the bathroom down the hall.

My feet on this floor should be in my own shoes.

I am admiring the colorful roses I have put in the dish or the cup.

I count the money. I have not gotten to the bathroom yet. I will.

I want to finish this up so I can get on with your life.

I do not want to have anything more to do with most of the other people.

You could be the one who is all so certain about what

somebody wants to do next, about what we should do next, if we should appear to be going to the bathroom next—at the same time, of course.

We should be certain. We should have no doubt.

Everything should feel natural, normal, and as if we were being swept off our feet.

Or at least mine.

Isn't this what you want?

❄ 35 ❄

If We Are Not Careful

Why do you think this is?

Say something!

If we are not careful, this could go on and on. We could stay in the bathroom whenever we get there—for a while.

This is not a good time to take a shit.

Now I am beginning to get worried.

I am worried.

I want your assurance.

I want your reassurance.

Perhaps I do not know what to do next, but everyone else does.

But do you know how to do anything under these circum-stances? You don't speak to me.

I close the bathroom door behind us. I appreciate the greatness of most of the articles in this room, whether we like it or not. Some of them were your idea.

The seventeenth-century pikeman is on loan from a relation.

I could tell you what I know about your possessions, because sometimes this ignites a tender feeling in both of us, I think.

Yes, there is tenderness here, and occasionally I forget why this is. Sorry.

✸ 36 ✸

Once I Had to Do
What I Had to Do

Of all of your favorites, I used to be the prettiest one. That's the kind of person I am. I have had some difficulty conning everybody, you first of all.

You are sauntering toward me.

Are you going to express an opinion?

I am the witness when you are silent or tedious.

I am a little worried. I am getting tired. I am getting sleepy. Hurry, hurry. You have to hurry. Can you hurry?

"Here, take these, too," I say, removing a few items from the hiding place.

You ask me, "Are you quite certain?"

Would you know how to find out?

"You are inspiring," you say, politely, I suppose.

Those are my instructions.

Pretty soon, one of us will leave the bathroom.

I think you will disapprove. You will think less of me. You will not like me. You won't like me anymore. You will stop liking me, which might impair the summer.

❦ 37 ❦

Please

Don't hate me when this is really all over. Do not go around saying crappy things about me.

Walking around outside, when the sunlight is brighter, we might enjoy this, don't you think?

Suddenly, a breeze will arrive, a lively breeze.

Please, this is not such a hardship to be such winsome people, because we are not in any trouble.

Returning now, to your inquiries, to your concerns, returning to anything that concerns you, you can take care of it, or just briefly consider how you could take care of it.

But briefly, it's always, I expect, too long.

❊ 38 ❊

The Events of the Morning Were Fairly Interesting

We could talk about it. Yes, your situation is certainly more of a monstrosity than mine is. Don't you have many more reasons to die than I do?

I admit everything gets easier and easier for me—as time goes by.

I get what I want when I want it. I have been, am, will be, well served.

We did get the celery soup. It's what I'd like, you know.

The events of the morning were fairly interesting. This is my news. We were on the toilet, you realize.

✳ 39 ✳

Everything Occurs as Planned

Everything occurs as planned. I am thrilled. I do not consider it poor taste to be this proud of a pair of shoes.

The shoes I am wearing are a recollection from your childhood.

"Don't you like them?" I say.

"They're so strange," you say.

❊ 40 ❊

Anytime of the Day or Evening

You have been taking advantage of some enjoyable moments. But you might be mistaken. Finally, you have come to believe that you should savor life. All of this adventure of ours has used up only about thirty-five minutes.

Time for our copulation.

I feel so amorous, but only a colossal effort has entitled me to feel this way.

"Please don't. Please," you beg me.

You have more than one deep, oozing starting point, it looks like. How did this happen?

You give me a playful kick. My foot is on you.

Why don't you let me stand on you even fleetingly?
Should I remember this?
Is there any reason to remember this?
To remember you? Oh—

❈ 41 ❈

Hasn't Someone Done This Thinking for Us?

Hasn't someone done this thinking for us?

Look out!

"Sorry."

Will you get away from these discomforts? The smell of mice? The plain ordinary dirtiness of my wanting to push yours or my filthy hair around, without my having to have one tremor of sensation?

I am ardent in the afternoon.

Perhaps I am a smaller, darker person than what you had in mind.

So sorry if you are not completely happy.

Be assured this repulsive moment is coming.

It is not safely past.

Nor passed.

❧ 42 ❧

This Time You Say No

You just want to be here with me.

The temperature of the room is cool. I want to pet you, but not your private part. I would not touch it with a fork.

You would think if I could tolerate the bedside clock that I could bind up your parcel with the cord!

They did not know why I felt this way.

You saw my nakedness. You had a great deal to worry about, even if I had made much of bathing daily. Yet you treated me courteously. You told me that you wanted me to remain in good cheer.

I was given a washing, which nearly fortified me. I was

fed the right foods. Let me tell you it will take much more strength to stop my pleasure in the nick of time than what I now have.

I forget—where did you say came from?

No, come.

Why don't you answer me?

Here is my solution that could help you anytime anywhere. Here is my advice, even though many of you consider me to be unclean.

Sweetness! Something wonderful will happen to you, which will make me happy!

They can keep remembering this—even if we do not.

❈ 43 ❈

We Could Fix an Egg

I could do something so that you and I would not be invited back.

You are better-looking than I am, better prepared, better behaved.

I do not like these men as much as I know I am supposed to.

I am so glad there are no little girls here. I would loathe it if there were little girls here. Older women give me that sense that I have value, but little girls make me feel like shit.

We could fix an egg.

Don't keep saying that! I don't agree. Don't tell me what to do!

❧ 44 ❧

A Necessity Arises

I am the one who tells you what to think.

We are very similar to people who stay together who do not really love each other but who want to love each other so much.

A necessity arises which has caused both of us to tremble all over. We—nobody could say why this is.

We could give this necessity the wretched synopsis it deserves: The Story of Our Lives.

One never knows, not for a thousand years, the way to speak to a woman such as I am, one who wears such footwear, who goes into the courtyard, who reposes at the fire, who undertakes the tasks—the tufts, the hollows—it is indescribable.

What if she even knew what she was doing when she cooked almost every vegetable available? Fruit is what she claims she likes. The liar.

The sounds on the roof could be scuffling, if it is a good night. We hear its goodness.

Some human beings do not hurt people, or damage property. They do not intensely glow, or become indivisible by merely looking at you.

To learn more about them, people should use you.

DALKEY ARCHIVE PAPERBACKS

FELIPE ALFAU, *Chromos.*
Locos.
Sentimental Songs.
ALAN ANSEN,
Contact Highs: Selected Poems 1957-1987.
DJUNA BARNES, *Ladies Almanack.*
Ryder.
JOHN BARTH, *LETTERS.*
Sabbatical.
ANDREI BITOV, *Pushkin House.*
ROGER BOYLAN, *Killoyle.*
CHRISTINE BROOKE-ROSE, *Amalgamemnon.*
GERALD BURNS, *Shorter Poems.*
MICHEL BUTOR,
Portrait of the Artist as a Young Ape.
JULIETA CAMPOS, *The Fear of Losing Eurydice.*
ANNE CARSON, *Eros the Bittersweet.*
LOUIS-FERDINAND CÉLINE, *Castle to Castle.*
North.
Rigadoon.
HUGO CHARTERIS, *The Tide Is Right.*
JEROME CHARYN, *The Tar Baby.*
EMILY HOLMES COLEMAN, *The Shutter of Snow.*
ROBERT COOVER, *A Night at the Movies.*
STANLEY CRAWFORD,
Some Instructions to My Wife.
RENÉ CREVEL, *Putting My Foot in It.*
RALPH CUSACK, *Cadenza.*
SUSAN DAITCH, *Storytown.*
PETER DIMOCK,
A Short Rhetoric for Leaving the Family.
COLEMAN DOWELL, *Island People.*
Too Much Flesh and Jabez.
RIKKI DUCORNET, *The Fountains of Neptune.*
The Jade Cabinet.
Phosphor in Dreamland.
The Stain.

WILLIAM EASTLAKE, *Lyric of the Circle Heart.*
STANLEY ELKIN, *The Dick Gibson Show.*
ANNIE ERNAUX, *Cleaned Out.*
LAUREN FAIRBANKS, *Muzzle Thyself.*
Sister Carrie.
LESLIE A. FIEDLER,
Love and Death in the American Novel.
RONALD FIRBANK, *Complete Short Stories.*
FORD MADOX FORD, *The March of Literature.*
JANICE GALLOWAY, *Foreign Parts.*
The Trick Is to Keep Breathing.
WILLIAM H. GASS,
Willie Masters' Lonesome Wife.
C. S. GISCOMBE, *Giscome Road.*
Here.
KAREN ELIZABETH GORDON, *The Red Shoes.*
GEOFFREY GREEN, ET AL, *The Vineland Papers.*
PATRICK GRAINVILLE, *The Cave of Heaven.*
JOHN HAWKES, *Whistlejacket.*
ALDOUS HUXLEY, *Antic Hay.*
Point Counter Point.
Those Barren Leaves.
Time Must Have a Stop.
TADEUSZ KONWICKI, *The Polish Complex.*
EWA KURYLUK, *Century 21.*
OSMAN LINS,
The Queen of the Prisons of Greece.
ALF MAC LOCHLAINN,
The Corpus in the Library.
Out of Focus.
D. KEITH MANO, *Take Five.*
BEN MARCUS, *The Age of Wire and String.*
DAVID MARKSON, *Collected Poems.*
Reader's Block.
Springer's Progress.
Wittgenstein's Mistress.
CARL R. MARTIN, *Genii Over Salzburg.*

Visit our website at www.cas.ilstu.edu/english/dalkey/dalkey.html

⊑
DALKEY ARCHIVE PAPERBACKS

CAROLE MASO, *AVA*.
HARRY MATHEWS, *20 Lines a Day*.
    Cigarettes.
    The Conversions.
    The Journalist.
    Tlooth.
JOSEPH MCELROY, *Women and Men*.
ROBERT L. MCLAUGHLIN, ED., *Innovations: An Anthology of Modern & Contemporary Fiction*.
JAMES MERRILL, *The (Diblos) Notebook*.
STEVEN MILLHAUSER, *The Barnum Museum*.
    In the Penny Arcade.
OLIVE MOORE, *Spleen*.
STEVEN MOORE, *Ronald Firbank: An Annotated Bibliography*.
NICHOLAS MOSLEY, *Accident*.
    Assassins.
    Children of Darkness and Light.
    Impossible Object.
    Judith.
    Natalie Natalia.
WARREN F. MOTTE, JR., *Oulipo*.
YVES NAVARRE, *Our Share of Time*.
WILFRIDO D. NOLLEDO, *But for the Lovers*.
FLANN O'BRIEN, *At Swim-Two-Birds*.
    The Dalkey Archive.
    The Hard Life.
    The Poor Mouth.
FERNANDO DEL PASO, *Palinuro of Mexico*.
RAYMOND QUENEAU, *The Last Days*.
    Pierrot Mon Ami.
REYOUNG, *Unbabbling*.
JULIÁN RÍOS, *Poundemonium*.
JACQUES ROUBAUD,
    The Great Fire of London.
    The Plurality of Worlds of Lewis.
    The Princess Hoppy.

LEON S. ROUDIEZ, *French Fiction Revisited*.
SEVERO SARDUY, *Cobra* and *Maitreya*.
ARNO SCHMIDT, *Collected Stories*.
    Nobodaddy's Children.
JUNE AKERS SEESE,
    Is This What Other Women Feel Too?
    What Waiting Really Means.
VIKTOR SHKLOVSKY, *Theory of Prose*.
JOSEF SKVORECKY, *The Engineer of Human Souls*.
CLAUDE SIMON, *The Invitation*.
GILBERT SORRENTINO, *Aberration of Starlight*.
    Imaginative Qualities of Actual Things.
    Mulligan Stew.
    Pack of Lies.
    The Sky Changes.
    Splendide-Hôtel.
    Steelwork.
    Under the Shadow.
W. M. SPACKMAN, *The Complete Fiction*.
GERTRUDE STEIN, *The Making of Americans*.
    A Novel of Thank You.
ALEXANDER THEROUX, *The Lollipop Trollops*.
ESTHER TUSQUETS, *Stranded*.
LUISA VALENZUELA, *He Who Searches*.
PAUL WEST,
    Words for a Deaf Daughter and *Gala*.
CURTIS WHITE,
    Memories of My Father Watching TV.
    Monstrous Possibility.
DIANE WILLIAMS, *Excitability: Selected Stories*.
DOUGLAS WOOLF, *Wall to Wall*.
PHILIP WYLIE, *Generation of Vipers*.
MARGUERITE YOUNG, *Angel in the Forest*.
    Miss MacIntosh, My Darling.
LOUIS ZUKOFSKY, *Collected Fiction*.
SCOTT ZWIREN, *God Head*.

Visit our website at www.cas.ilstu.edu/english/dalkey/dalkey.html

Dalkey Archive Press
ISU Campus Box 4241, Normal, IL 61790–4241
fax (309) 438–7422